THE BEATLES GRAPHIC

HERVÉ BOURHIS

OMNIBUS PRESS

LONDON / NEW YORK / PARIS / SYDNEY / COPENHAGEN / BERLIN / MADRID / HONG KONG / TOKYO

Copyright © 2010 Dargaud
This edition copyright © 2012 Omnibus Press
(A Division of Music Sales Limited)

Graphics by Hervé Bourhis & Phillipe Ravon
Cover designed by Liz Barrand
Translated from French by Paul Buck & Catherine Petit

ISBN: 978.1.78038.156.5
Order No: OP54296

Exclusive Distributors
Music Sales Limited,
14/15 Berners Street,
London, W1T 3LJ.

Music Sales Corporation,
257 Park Avenue South,
New York, NY 10010, USA.

Macmillan Distribution Services,
56 Parkwest Drive
Derrimut, Vic 3030,
Australia.

Printed in Croatia.

A catalogue record for this book is available from the British Library.
Visit Omnibus Press on the web at www.omnibuspress.com

PREFACE

After his *Little Book Of Rock*, an illustrated handbook as healthily subjective as it was joyfully erudite about a life devoted to the binary rhythm, Hervé Bourhis does it again. Now he's focused his pencil on the most mythical band of them all, whose every song has become a classic, the Beatles. And his magic works again. The epic story of the four boys from Liverpool, from their prehistory to the final recordings by the two surviving members, unfolds as the most incredible roller-coaster succession of triumphs and inventions, complicities and betrayals, harmonies and disagreements the world has ever seen. Charismatic, clever, facetious, arrogant and, of course, brimming with talent, John, Paul, George and Ringo took on that world and won. The story reads like a matrix of all the subsequent adventures in rock, from the most public to the most private and, herein, is given a new twist through Hervé Bourhis' unique point of view. Hervé is a very special fan, obsessive but objective, passionate but not blind, whose imagination has been shaped by the images, the iconic albums sleeves, movies and photographs, as much as by the words and music. His perception of the legendary Far Four, affectionately unpretentious yet sincere and precise, miraculously refreshes our own preconceptions about the greatest pop group ever.

Hugo Cassavetti

INTRODUCTION TO ENGLISH EDITION

I've loved the *Magical Mystery Tour* album since 1989. I bought the tape because I didn't have a CD player and it was practical for listening to on the bus to school. A year later I bought the vinyl because it was a beautiful object, with a thick booklet full of pictures from the film.

When I met my partner Alexandra, she had the CD. Then, for my 33rd birthday, she gave me the original vinyl, the famous 1967 double EP. Last year, I transferred the CD onto my MP3.

I still listen to that old tape in my car. It seems to keep going, even though it no longer looks that great.

This book is my attempt at paying tribute to the Beatles. Even though I've listened to other artists since I was 15, I always return to them when I don't know what else to listen to.

Hervé Bourhis.

ACKNOWLEDGEMENTS

Thanks to: François Ayroles, Cleet Boris, Christian Durieux, Christophe Gaultier, Pascal Girard, Klaus Humann, David Scrima and Rudy Spiessert for their unpublished drawings, scattered throughout the book.

Thanks also to Mme Beaumenay-Joannet, Monsieur Stanislas Barthelemy, Mme Anne Goscinny, Monsieur Marcel Gotlib, Monsieur Albert Uderzo.

And also: Catherine Bazabas, Elliott and Pierre, Fabien Bourhis, Sandrine Capelle, Thierry ("the spotter"), Carl-Stéphane Georgin, Frédéric Gerbault, Claudia Jerusalem-Groenewald, Olivier Jouvray, Xavier Ladousse, Dominique Luczack, Philippe Ostermann, Alexandra Philips (Greatest Maccafan alive), Laurent Rullier and Sylvian Yon for their support.

Editor's note to UK edition: As this book was originally intended for a French audience it contains references of a French nature that might seem slightly incongruous to English and American Beatle fans. Mostly, after translation, they have been left as the (French) author intended. There have been hundreds of Beatle books written by authors whose first language is English and whose point of view was informed by how The Beatles were perceived in Britain and the USA. This one is slightly different.

ENTRANCE TO MERSEY TUNNEL

AERIAL VIEW

THE CATHEDRAL

GREETINGS FROM
LIVERPOOL

CLAYTON SQUARE

MERSEY AND ROYAL LIVER BUILDING

Liverpool
Merseyside

LIVERPOOL

ENGLAND

Liverpool is a city port in the North-west of England.

DEUS nobis   HOEC   otia fecit

Liverpool's coat-of-arms incorporates its symbol, the liver bird.

Liverpool in five dates:
- 1207:
Creation of the city.
- 18th century:
Trade with the West Indies (41% of the
European trade in slaves).
- 1851:
Thanks to its port, the "British
New York" is richer and more dynamic
than London.
- 1908-1912:
Building of the Titanic.
- 1940:
Around 900,000 inhabitants
(fifth city in England).

In Liverpool,
the terrible bombings
of 1940 and 1941
are responsible
for thousands of deaths.
Parts of the city are destroyed.

Blitz

1940

Richard and Elsie
take pleasure
in announcing
the birth of their son
Richard Henry Parkin Starkey Jr.
on July 7
in Madryn Street, Liverpool (the Dingle).

On October 9,
during a German air raid
and in a complete blackout,
Julia Lennon (born Stanley)
gives birth to
John Winston Lennon
at Oxford St
Maternity Hospital.

"Winston"
is chosen
by Julia
as a tribute
to Churchill.

Winston Churchill

Winston Churchill visits the EMI studios in Abbey Road,
London. Jokingly, he asks the technicians dressed in white
lab coats: "I must be in the wrong place. Is this a hospital?"

1942

June 18:
James Paul McCartney is born at the Walton General Hospital in Liverpool, son of Jim (cotton salesman and amateur musician) and Mary (nurse and midwife).

Of Irish origin, McCartney is written without the "a" in "Mac", and as one word, with a capital for "Cartney".

SCOUSE!

IS THE LIVERPOOL ACCENT, NOT JUST A WAY OF SPEAKING BUT A REFLECTION OF THE HUMOUR AND SPIRIT OF ITS PEOPLE.

43

February 25:
George Harrison is born at his parents' home, 12 Arnold Grove (Wavetree), a small terraced house with an outside toilet at the rear.

George is the youngest of four children.

WHITE STAR LINE

His father, Harold Hargreaves Harrison, is a bus driver and was a ship's steward on the White Star Line. His mother, Louise, is a housewife.

45

George Martin volunteers to fight with the Royal Air Force.

He is 19.

Alfred "Freddy" Lennon, separated from Julia, has spent the last few years at sea. He returns and decides to take his son John with him to New Zealand, but John chooses to stay with his mother.

The young John Lennon likes to play in the gardens of the old orphanage belonging to the Salvation Army.

STRAWBERRY FIELD

46

Little Richard Starkey's health is a worry. After a bout of peritonitis, he remains in a coma for 10 weeks.

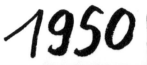

After graduating from the Guildhall School of Music, George Martin joins EMI as assistant to the head of the Parlophone label.

Yoko Ono, 20 years old, the daughter of a rich Japanese family exiled since the war, starts at the Sarah Lawrence College, a very chic and liberal Art School situated near New York.

Richard Starkey spends another six months at the hospital, compromising his schooling

1950

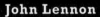

John Lennon

starts at Quarry Bank High School. He is a curious and creative boy who writes poems inspired by Lewis Carroll (notably The Jabberwocky). He has been living for seven years now with his aunt Mimi in Woolton, an upmarket area of Liverpool. She is the sister of Julia who has decided not to keep him because her new boyfriend, John Dykins, is unwilling to raise another man's child.

53

Paul McCartney, now at Joseph Williams Primary School, wins First Prize in a local competition to mark the coronation. In his essay he praises the monarchy.

Paul meets George (here with Grandma Harrison) on the school bus. They go to the same school, but Paul treats him like a little boy even though the gap in their ages is only nine months.

Brian Epstein, 19 years old, has his military service reduced due to his homosexuality. He is asked to return home because of "mental and emotional incompatibility". In reality, he dressed as an officer to chase boys in London bars, and was denounced.

THE WILD ONE

"ALL THE BEETLES MISS YA" SAYS LEE MARVIN TO MARLON BRANDO. THE "BEETLES" ARE THE GIRLS OF THE MOTORCYCLE GANG IN THIS FAMOUS FILM.

Hofner

Hofner invents the 500/1 violin bass.

54 Julia Lennon

sees her son John again, and teaches him (rather badly) the rudiments of guitar.

John sings and plays banjo and ukulele.

TRADE *Parlophone* MARK
MADE IN ENGLAND

George Martin becomes manager of the Parlophone label, which releases classical, baroque, traditional folk music and comedy (like the Goon Show, with Peter Sellers).

The young Harrison, who loves speed, is disappointed when Juan Manuel Fangio comes second to Sterling Moss at the British GP Aintree course, near Liverpool.

Death of George Smith, the husband of Aunt Mimi, whom John considered his father.

Before his death, he had given John a Hohner chromatic harmonica.

55

56

Mary McCartney dies of breast cancer. "I would love to have seen the boys growing up," are her last words. Jim and his two sons, Paul (14) and Michael (12), are totally distraught.

In *Rushworth & Dreapers*, Paul sells the trumpet he had been given. He buys a guitar (a Zenith). Left-handed, he reverses the strings.

He composes his first song 'I Lost My Little Girl'.

TEDDY BOYS

1956 IS THE YEAR WHEN THE ENGLISH YOUTH DISCOVER ROCK'N'ROLL THANKS TO RADIO LUXEMBOURG.

LIVERPOOL IS AT THE FOREFRONT.

BUT THE RECORDS ARE RARE AND EXPENSIVE.

THE FIRST ROCK SONG HEARD BY GEORGE HARRISON.

Aunt Mimi throws away John's poems. He tells her: "You've thrown my poetry out and you'll regret it when I'm famous."

mimi

IMPERIAL

XS386

I'M IN LOVE AGAIN

FATS DOMINO
IM-233

"Lennon" is a Gaelic name of Irish origin (like 25% of Liverpudlians). There is also a village called Lennon in France (Finistère).

BIOLETTI
• Barber •
• Hairdresser •

Penny Lane, Liverpool

'ROCK WITH THE CAVEMAN' BY TOMMY STEELE IS THE FIRST ENGLISH ROCK SONG.

DECCA RECORDS

TOMMY STEELE
Young Love

YOUNG LOVE • DOOMSDAY ROCK • WEDDING BELLS • ROCK WITH THE CAVEMAN

RICHARD BUYS HIS FIRST SNARE DRUM.

57 January 16: opening of the Cavern Club at 19 Mathew Street, Liverpool.

John Lennon forms The Quarrymen, a skiffle group. The name comes from his school, the Quarry Bank Grammar School. The members are:

JOHN ELNNON
BILL SMITH
ERIC GRIFFITHS
ROD DAVIS
PETE SHOTTON
COLIN HANTON

Skiffle is very popular with English youth, mainly because it requires only home-made and thus cheap instruments: a washboard is used for percussion, and a broomstick with a string, fixed to a tea-chest, is the bass.

Woolton garden fete July 6

Paul goes to The Quarrymen's gig with his friend Ivan. He likes their rock covers and notices "a guy up on the stage wearing a checked shirt". After the gig, Ivan introduces Paul to John. Paul plays 'Twenty Flight Rock' with the right chords and words, which impresses John.

GARDEN FETE
ST. PETER'S CHURCH FIELD

WOOLTON PARISH CHURCH

Saturday, 6th July, 1957
at 3 p.m.
Admission by Programme
CHILDREN 3d.

PROCEED IN AID OF CHURCH FUNDS

July 8 or 9: Pete Shotton tells Paul that John wants him in the Quarrymen. "Okay, but after the holidays," says Paul.

CHESS
RECORD CORP

You like

Perhaps you might like:

414

"ROCK AND ROLL MUSIC"
(C. BERRY)
CHUCK BERRY
1671

MADE BY CHESS RECORDS CORP. CHICAGO, ILL.

john & Paul.

After checking out each other for a while, the two teenagers become very close. Though very different in personality, they share the same tastes. Paul teaches John chords. They begin writing songs together in the McCartneys' living room. The first is called 'Too Bad About Sorrows'.

John and Paul steal a record by the Coasters from the home of a friend.

Richard Starkey co-founds the

Ed Clayton Skiffle Group.

(By day he does odd jobs.)

THE FRIENDS OF MY FRIENDS...

Ivan Vaughn, Paul McCartney's best friend.

Pete Shotton, John Lennon's best friend.

George Harrison, 14, draws guitars in the margins of his exercise books. His mother ends up buying one for him.

John enters Liverpool Art College.

November 23 Quarrymen's 'concert' at the New Clubmoor Hall.

Paul has joined the band a month earlier.

The members are Colin Hanton, Paul McCartney, Len Garry, John Lennon, Eric Griffiths.

NEMS

58

In February, at Paul's suggestion, George Harrison joins The Quarrymen, despite John's objections (George is only 15). But hey, he knows Duane Eddy's 'Raunchy' note for note, which plays in his favour.

Buddy Holly and the Crickets

CORAL
941 23 15 K∅M-

Oh Boy! • Words of Love
Peggy Sue • I'm looking for someone to love

You like

Perhaps you might like:

Recorded by P. F. PHILLIPS

KENSINGTON

IN SPITE OF ALL THE DANGER

Play with a light-weight Pick-up

(McCartney, Harrison)

July 14: first recording by The Quarrymen at Percy Phillips' studio in Liverpool. For 17/6d, an acetate is made of Buddy Holly's 'That'll Be The Day' and 'In Spite Of All The Danger', their own composition. Each musician is allowed to keep it at home for a week, taking turns.

Paul writes 'When I'm 64' alone, and 'Love Me Do' with John.

Menlove Avenue.

July 15: Julia Lennon dies after being run down by an off-duty policeman, who is found blameless.

John, traumatised, becomes uncontrollable and takes to drinking.

Richard who prefers to be called Ritchie, becomes drummer for RAVING TEXAS.

John begins a complicated relationship with Cynthia Powell, a classmate from Art School.

59

John meets **Stuart Sutcliffe** in a pub near the Art School. Stuart is a promising young painter, slightly older than John, and handsome in a mysterious James Dean way.

They become close friends, which makes Paul and George jealous.

George, here dressed for a wedding, has left school. He becomes an electrician for a few weeks.

CASBAH CLUB

ROCK 'N' ROLL   SKIFFLE

The Quarry Men

OPEN FOR ENGAGEMENTS   MANAGER GATEACRE 1715

August/September: several concerts by The Quarrymen at Liverpool's Casbah Club, owned by the dynamic Mona Best. The club is in the basement of her own house.

Rory Storm AND HIS HURRICANES

Richard Starkey joins the professional group Rory Storm & The Hurricanes, led by the charismatic Alan Caldwell.

The Maharishi Mahesh Yogi, disciple of the famous Swami Brahmananda Saraswati, founds the movement of Transcendental Meditation, destined for the Western world.

October 31:
The Quarrymen, renamed **JOHNNY & THE MOONDOGS**, audition for the Carol Lewis Show.

They fail.

Whose turn to be drummer now?

Specialty
45 RPM

KANSAS CITY
(Leiber-Stoller)
LITTLE RICHARD
664

You like THE QUARRYMEN
Perhaps you might like:

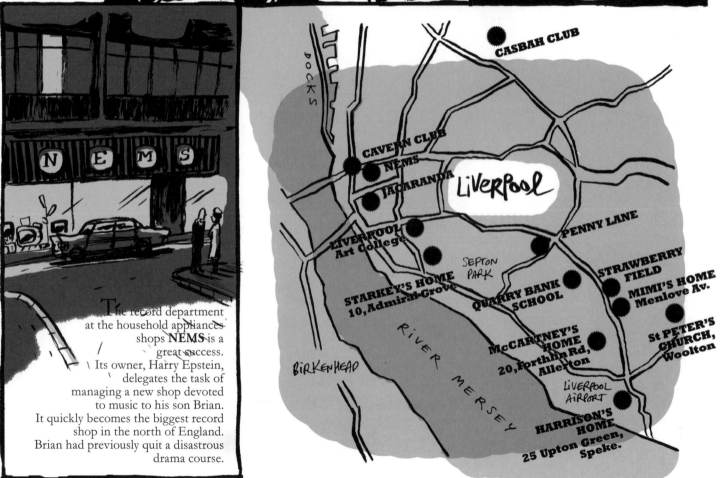

The record department at the household appliances shops **NEMS** is a great success.
Its owner, Harry Epstein, delegates the task of managing a new shop devoted to music to his son Brian.
It quickly becomes the biggest record shop in the north of England. Brian had previously quit a disastrous drama course.

DOCKS

CASBAH CLUB

CAVERN CLUB
NEMS
JACARANDA

LiVERPOOL

LIVERPOOL
Art College

PENNY LANE

SEFTON PARK

STARKEY'S HOME
10, Admiral Grove

QUARRY BANK
SCHOOL

STRAWBERRY FIELD

MIMI'S HOME
Menlove Av.

McCARTNEY'S HOME
20, Forthlin Rd,
Allerton

St PETER'S CHURCH,
Woolton

BIRKENHEAD

RIVER MERSEY

LIVERPOOL AIRPORT

HARRISON'S HOME
25 Upton Green,
Speke.

Rickenbacker 325
(1958)

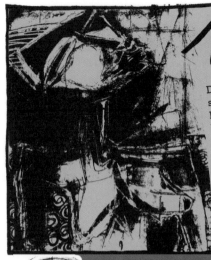

1960

During an exhibition, Stu sells his first painting. John, Paul and George convince him to buy a bass and join the band, though he would have preferred to buy painting materials with the money.

A mediocre bass player, he plays mainly with his back to the audience, the volume turned down.

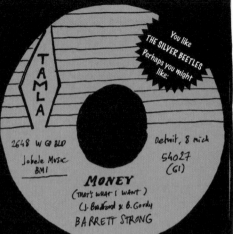

You like THE SILVER BEETLES Perhaps you might like:

TAMLA

2648 W GD BLD
Jobele Music
BMI

Detroit, 8 mich
54027
(G1)

MONEY
(THAT'S WHAT I WANT)
(J. Bradford & B. Gordy
BARRETT STRONG

YOUR COUNTRY DOESN'T NEED YOU

End of military service in the United Kingdom. A whole generation of musicians escapes conscription.

Neil Aspinall, a school friend of Paul and George, becomes their road manager.

THE QUARRYMEN ARE RENAMED
THE SILVER BEETLES
(like Buddy Holly's Crickets, but as beetles) and adopt the pseudonyms:

LONG JOHN!
PAUL RAMON!
CARL HARRISON!
STU DE STAËL!

August 15: Pete Best, the son of the Casbah Club's owner, becomes the drummer for the Silver Beetles.

Long John & the Silver Beetles

Our young friends want to become professional.

Allan Williams, the manager of their favourite coffee bar, the Jacaranda, becomes their manager. He arranges a tour of Scotland accompanying Johnny Gentle, an unrewarding and discouraging experience. They had been promised Billy Fury, the star of Liverpudlian rock.

August 16: The band (and their van) arrive in Hamburg for a series of concerts.

Hamburg, 1960.
Große Freiheit

Ex-clown Bruno Koschmider likes to hire bands from Liverpool to liven up his nightclubs in the red district of Sankt Pauli.

BAMBI KINO

In the shabby dressing room of this decrepit cinema our friends sleep with an old Union Jack as blanket.

Hamburg represents a complete loss of innocence for our provincial young men: the vibrant clubs, the violence of drunk audiences, the amphetamines (Preludin) to stay awake all night, and sex with prostitutes.

Around August 16, 1960, John and Stuart find a new name for their group:

THE BEATLES.

INDRA

The Beatles play every night for five to six hours. They perfect a repertoire of rock'n'roll standards and their own compositions. They gradually become a solid and wild stage band.

Astrid Kirchherr

Klaus Voorman

EXIS

Klaus Voorman, an art and illustration student, meets The Beatles by chance at the Kaiserkeller. Fascinated, he returns with his friends Astrid Kirchherr and Jürgen Vollmer. They become fans and friends of The Beatles who, in turn, admire these bohemian and sophisticated "exis" (existentialists).

**NOVEMBER 1960
HEILIGENGEISTFELD SQUARE
(PHOTOS ASTRID KIRCHHERR)**

KAISERKELLER
Tanzpalast der Jugend
HAMBURG-ST.PAULI
präsentiert Bruno Koschmider
ORIGINAL
Rock'n Roll
BANDS
Rory Storm
AND HIS HURICAN
und
the Beatles
ENGLAND · LIVERPOOL

Because of his rings and his famous "Starr time" (a drum solo he performs at each show), Richard Starkey chooses to be called RINGO STARR.

Ausfahrt!

November 21:
Two Beatles deported from Germany!

George - because he isn't old enough to work legally in a nightclub.
Paul - for almost setting fire to the Bambi Kino (by burning a condom).
In reality, Bruno Koschmider didn't want the Beatles to play in a rival club and denounced them.

They all return to Liverpool discouraged.

Make a Show!

* "SET FIRE"
(Bruno Koschmider's advise)

1. John Lennon, arched, legs spread, short-sighted like a mole

2. A member of the infamous Hoddel's Gang, ex-boxers who become bouncers

3. Stu, decorative element

4. Pete Best, metronome

5. Paul McCartney, drinking, eating, smoking

61

STU has remained in Hamburg with Astrid. She has set up a studio for him in the attic of her parents' home. He will still play occasionally with the Beatles, but in reality he's no longer part of the group.

Spring 1961: The Beatles return for a series of concerts in Hamburg's clubs. After a few gigs on piano, Paul ends up buying a Hofner 'Violin' bass guitar.

February 12: Casbah Club. Paul, skint, puts four piano strings on his old Rosetti "Solid 7" and becomes the Beatles' bass player.

with "a"!

"It came in a vision – a man appeared on a Flaming Pie and said unto them 'From this day on you are Beatles with an A'."

John Lennon, the July 6, 1961 edition of Merseybeat, a Liverpudlian music magazine.

First Beatles fan-club in Liverpool.

BAMBI KINO

Große Freiheit

INDRA STAR CLUB KAISERKELLER

Astrid's place.

Photos of waste land.

Hamburg

TOP TEN CLUB (Reeperbahn)

SANKT PAULI

THE DOCKS

'Cry For A Shadow'.
A pastiche of The Shadows, credited to Harrison-Lennon, is recorded during the sessions with Tony Sheridan.

TONY SHERIDAN
POLYDOR
24 673

My Bonnie

THE SAINTS
(WHEN THE SAINTS GO MARCHING IN)

John Lennon

April 1961.

TONY SHERIDAN & THE BEAT BROTHERS
My Bonnie / The Saints

Single/October 1961/Polydor

"Beatles" sounds too much like "Peedles" (small boy's penis in German). Under the name "Beat Brothers" our friends accompany Tony Sheridan on a single of little interest beyond the fact that it's the Beatles' first professional record. Or the Beat Brothers. With Tony Sheridan. Or the opposite.

A Bert Kaempfert production, recorded in Hamburg.

'My Bonnie' reaches fifth place in the German hit parade. It establishes Tony Sheridan, that rocker from Liverpool, as a regular in Hamburg's clubs.

In the Top Ten, on top of the Beatles concerts, and for a week, Paul takes over for Tony Sheridan's drummer, who is ill.

In Hamburg, the Beatles become good friends with Ringo Starr, the drummer in the Hurricanes.

Stu has a new hairstyle based on Jean-Claude Brialy, cut by Astrid. George copies him, despite being mocked by the others.

PARIS!

For his 21st Birthday, thanks to Mimi's gift of 100, John spends two weeks in Paris with Paul and Jurgen, the latter giving them a "French" hairstyle.

A revolution for those hair-slicked-back rockers.

"I was immediately struck by their music, their beat, and their sense of humour on stage - and, even afterwards, when I met them, I was struck again by their personal charm. And it was there that, really, it all started."

November 9: Brian Epstein comes to see the Beatles at the Cavern Club.

December 3

Epstein: Let's keep it simple. You need a manager: do you want me to be in charge?

Lennon : OK, Brian, manage us. Where's the contract?

Jean-Claude Brialy
Le Beau Serge
(Handsome Serge)
Chabrol, 1958

MERSEYSIDE'S OWN ENTERTAINMENTS PAPER

MERSEY BEAT

NEMS
WHITECHAPEL AND GREAT
CHARLOTTE STREET
THE FINEST RECORD SELEC-
TIONS IN THE NORTH
Open until 6.0 p.m. each day
(Thursday and Saturday 6.30 p.m.)

Vol. 1 No. 13   JANUARY 4-18, 1962   Price THREEPENC

Beatles   Top Poll!

FULL RESULTS INSIDE
Cover photograph by Albert Marrion

JOHN LENNON   GEORGE HARRISON   PAUL McARTREY   PETE BEST

January 1962
Brian Epstein lines up an audition with Decca Records.
Tired from touring, our friends are not on their best form. Decca turn them down. "Guitar bands are on their way out, Mr Epstein," says Dick Rowe. "You really should stick to selling records in Liverpool."
Epstein meets with refusal after refusal from the record labels, but never becomes discouraged. On the contrary, in Liverpool The Beatles are voted the city's best band.

WALTON LANE SOCIAL CLUB
Proprietor: Mrs. Ada Taylor
THE PULSE OF CLUBLAND
ALWAYS A WELCOME FOR
MEMBERS AND FRIENDS

N.U.R. No. 5 Social Club
DEANE ROAD, LIVERPOOL
Secretary: Mr. J. Ouigan
THE HAPPY CLUB
ONLY THE BEST IS GOOD
ENOUGH FOR OUR
MEMBERS AND FRIENDS

MERSEYSIDE CLUBS ASSOCIATION
Headquarters:

STU
SUTCLIFFE

(1940-1962)

On April 10, Stuart Sutcliffe, 21, dies in Hamburg of a brain haemorrhage. None of the Beatles attend his funeral.

Dick Rowe

The man from Decca who didn't sign the Beatles.

New rules decreed by Brian Epstein: it is forbidden to smoke, drink, eat or swear on stage. No more leather. Say hello to the audience.

As EMI fails to answer his letters, Epstein threatens to stop stocking their records in his shops. On May 9, George Martin listens to the tapes recorded at Decca. He is not impressed. Nevertheless he arranges an audition.

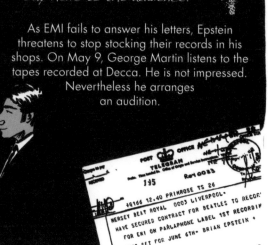

April 13 – 31 May
Fourth season in Hamburg.
The Beatles play at the newly opened
Star Club. Astrid, still faithful,
comes to see them, but alone.

Extremely talented organist,
aged 16, accompanist to Ray
Charles and Little Richard,
Billy befriends the Beatles
at the Star Club.

Billy Preston

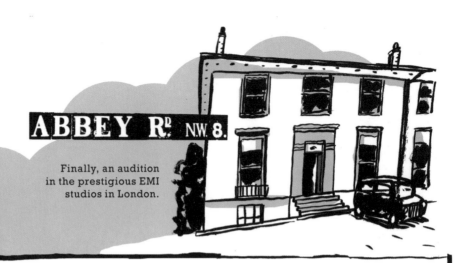

Finally, an audition
in the prestigious EMI
studios in London.

George Martin, head of the
Parlophone label, takes them
on a tour of the studios.

Martin: Look, I've
laid into you for
quite a time, you
haven't responded.
Is there anything
you don't like?

Harrison: Yeah,
I don't like your tie!

Martin, after the
audition, is not madly
enthusiastic, but
decides to sign
them, having
"nothing to lose".

July 1
At the
Cavern Club,
with their hero
Gene Vincent,
they dress in
leather for the
occasion.

Between June and
August, the Beatles
play around 30 times
at the Cavern,
sometimes two
concerts a day.
They really feel at
home there.

Bye-bye PETE BEST!

August 16
George Martin asks the Beatles to
change their drummer. They agree,
for Pete Best never shared the
other three's sense of humour or
even changed his Fifties hairstyle.
Brian Epstein is charged with giving
him the bad news.

Ringo has a natural white lock of hair.

Bingo!

August 18: at George Harrison's instigation, the Beatles choose their mate Ringo Starr as the new drummer.

John tells him: "Get rid of your beard, Ringo, and change your hairstyle."

CYNTHIA IS PREGNANT. JOHN MARRIES HER IMMEDIATELY. MIMI, WHO DOESN'T APPROVE OF THE RELATIONSHIP, STAYS AWAY FROM THE CEREMONY.

THIS AGREEMENT is made the 1st day of Oc... 1962 BETWEEN NEMW ENTERPRISES LIMITED whose Registered ... situate at 62/72 Walton Road in the city of Liverpool (h... called "the Manager) of the first part JOHN WINSTON LE... 251 Menlove Avenue GEORGE HARRISON of 25 Upton Green J... McCARTNEY of 20 Forthlin Road and RICHARD STARKEY of... all of Liverpool aforesaid (hereinafter called "the ... second part and HAROLD HEARGRAVES HARRISON of 25 Up... (hereinafter called "Mr. Harrison") JAMES McCARTNEY ... Road (hereinafter called "Mr. McCartney") both of Live...

A few days after Ringo joins, a fan of Pete Best punches George Harrison in the face. George sports his black eye on some promo photos.

RINGO NEVER! PETE BEST FOREVER!

Rebellion!

September 4 & 11

At the first recording sessions at Abbey Road Studios George Martin wants The Beatles to record 'How Do You Do It?' as their first single. They prefer 'Love Me Do', one of their own compositions.

In the end Martin gives in, surprised by the willpower of the young greenhorns.

But now he has Ringo in his bad books...

Andy White

On 'Love Me Do', George Martin replaces Ringo with Andy White, a true pro. But Ringo is the best drummer in Liverpool! the other three say, offended.

The Beatles' first TV appearance is broadcast live from the Cavern, on Granada, the commercial channel in northern England.

THE BEATLES
Love me do / P.S. I love you

Single/October 62/Parlophone

This is the first real Beatles single. 'Love Me Do' was composed by Paul in 1958. John's harmonica part made an impression at the time. It is all very charming, properly executed, but is a long way from the energy shown by the band on stage.

Brian Epstein orders 10,000 copies to make sure it reaches the charts. The single finishes at number 17 in the national charts, a genuine success for a first record by a group known only in the north of the country.

November 26: They record their second single. Ringo, humiliated in September, is accepted by George Martin this time.

Recorded but rejected: 'Tip Of My Tongue'.

Cruel joke: Using a pseudonym, George Martin sent a tape of 'Please Please Me', as yet unreleased, to Decca for an audition.

Did Decca refuse the Beatles a second time?

After her six-year marriage to composer Toshi Ichiyanagi, Yoko marries again, this time to Anthony Cox, a jazz musician and film producer.

Auf Wiedersehen Hamburg!

December 7: Their last trip to Hamburg. When they arrive, a giant banner and hundreds of fans are waiting near the Star Club. Even though they play support to Little Richard, their heart is no longer there. The years of seedy clubs are behind them.

63

JANUARY - FEBRUARY

The Beatles criss-cross the icy roads of England on their first theatre tour, headlined by Helen Shapiro.

February 11:
The first album is recorded in one day! Exhausted by touring and with John suffering from a cold and sore throat, they drink milk and suck on cough sweets for the entire session. Focused, they refuse lunch, re-working some songs. The last (and best), 'Twist And Shout', is recorded by John in one take.

John and Paul write all the time while touring, in hotel rooms, on the coach, anywhere they find themselves. Galvanised by the positive reception of 'Love Me Do', their ambition as composers seems limitless.

THE BEATLES
Please please me / Ask me why

Single/January 1963/Parlophone

"You've got your first Number One," George Martin predicts during the recording of 'Please Please Me', a song written by John while still a teenager. More dynamic and catchy than 'Love Me Do', the Beatles are at their best in the studio. The original version, inspired by Roy Orbison, was thought by Martin to have been too slow and mournful, so he suggests upping the tempo.

It was indeed their first number one.

Recorded but rejected: 'Hold Me Tight' and 'The One After 909'.

Northern Songs

is the name of the company founded by Dick James, Brian Epstein, John Lennon and Paul McCartney to manage the music publishing of the duo's songs.

The two Beatles sign the contract without reading it.

OFF THE BEATLE TRACK

This is the name George Martin suggests for their first album, which was to be a live recording from the Cavern Club. For the sleeve, Martin had envisaged a photo at London Zoo, in the insect house. But the Zoological Society of London refuses, finding the idea 'in bad taste'.

It could have looked something like this: →

April

Brian Epstein and John Lennon go on holiday to Spain, feeding rumours about their relationship…

… So John is absent from the birth of his son, John Charles Julian, on the April 8. Brian asks John not to tell the press, and to keep his marriage a secret too.

Brian Epstein's stable of artists monopolises the top places in the British charts. All Liverpudlians, Gerry & the Pacemakers, Cilla Black, Billy J.Kramer all sing McCartney/ Lennon compositions. Everyone is talking about Merseybeat.

"I have nothing against the Beatles, but in your last issue, I counted you mentioned them 79 times!"

(A reader of the New Musical Express)

Jane Asher

PAUL AND CHILD PRODIGY ACTRESS JANE ASHER (17 YEARS OLD, WITH AN 11 YEARS CAREER) BECOME "CLOSE FRIENDS".

FROM ME TO YOU
THANK YOU GIRL

THE BEATLES

Martin and Epstein's strategy: two albums a year and non-album singles four times a year.

Our friends leave Liverpool for London. Fans hang around in front of 57 Green Street, the flat they share…

THE BEATLES
From me to you / Thank you girl

Single/April 63/Parlophone

Hey presto! A new single is out, one month after the first album! 'From Me To You', written by John & Paul, gets its inspiration from the NME's readers' page. Far from being one of the major songs by the duo, its delicious bridge saves it from banality, and its very shrill "woo" marks an important moment.

This single dislodges 'How Do You Do It?' by Gerry & the Pacemakers, the song they had declined to record, from number one in the charts.

Dezo Hoffmann's iconic photos and the collarless suits designed by Douglas Millings mark the end of the wild years. Astrid Kirchherr says she doesn't recognize "her Beatles", whose image has been shaped by Brian Epstein for maximum mass appeal – but not without the willing agreement of the four boys.

4,000 fans

without tickets provoke a riot in front of Blackpool's Queen's Theatre.

August 1963

The first *Beatles Book Monthly* is published, a magazine for fans, retracing the story and movements of the quartet with their co-operation and that of Brian Epstein. Sean Mahoney, alias Johnny Dean, prints 110,000 copies of the first issue. Immediate success.

On July 1, a horde of hysterical fans manage to enter the EMI studios, chasing after the Beatles. The young girls are brought under control. The boys, still in shock, carry on recording of 'She Loves You'. The security of the studio has to be beefed up and now resembles a bunker.

August 3.
Final appearance at the Cavern Club.

THE BEATLES

SHE LOVES YOU

I'LL GET YOU

R 5055 PARLOPHONE

THE BEATLES
She loves you / I'll get you

Single/August 63/Parlophone

Opening with a short tom-tom roll, the chorus comes charging in like a double-decker bus topped with a Mersey wig.

Two minutes and 22 seconds of pure teenage energy later, the listener is generally KO-ed and euphoric.

Number one straight away. One million singles sold in England alone.
Their first gold disc.

Yeah Yeah Yeah.

MAL EVANS,
the giant-sized ex-doorman of the Cavern, becomes roadie, driver and bodyguard for the band, while Neil Aspinall becomes tour manager.

My tailor is rich.

Douglas Millings, 63 Old Compton Street, Soho.

He creates the collarless jackets inspired by Pierre Cardin.

Competition arrives!!

THE ROLLING STONES ARE SOLD BY THEIR MANAGER ANDREW OLDHAM AS THE ANTI-BEATLES. MICK JAGGER CALLS OUR FRIENDS "THE FOUR-HEADED MONSTER"! NEVERTHELESS OLDHAM ASKS JOHN AND PAUL FOR A NEW SONG AND IS OFFERED "I WANNA BE YOUR MAN" AS THEIR SECOND SINGLE.

"WE WEREN"T GOING TO GIVE THEM ANYTHING GREAT, RIGHT?" LENNON SAID LATER.

with the beatles

PARLOPHONE

mono

THE BEATLES
With the Beatles

LP/November 63/Parlophone

Eight months have passed since the first album and everything has changed. From the era of the Cavern(s) to With The Beatles, the group has become a phenomenon.

With the help of George Martin, they have developed their sound into more sophisticated areas.

Eight new compositions and six covers (often Motown) all demonstrate more coherence and control.

'All My Loving' and 'Not A Second Time' reveal a talent for composition which belies their age and sets a new yardstick in style. The Beatles have also taken control of their image, using photographer Robert Freeman to take a cover shot which recreates the crepuscular atmosphere of Astrid Kirchherr's photographs.

This classy, artistic sleeve is a first as far as music destined for teenagers is concerned. **"We are artists, not a fashion,"** it seems to say.

With The Beatles replaces *Please Please Me* on top of the LP charts. It becomes the second million selling LP record in Great Britain, at a time when these figures usually remained confidential.

When the very respectable Sir Joseph Lockwood, boss of EMI, presents the Beatles with a silver record, he makes a mistake in his speech. Having a laugh, Lennon says: "YOU'RE FIRED!"

Paul moves into the chic townhouse of Jane Asher's parents in Wimpole Street, living in an attic room. He benefits from the intellectual atmosphere that reigns in the home and finds himself a new family.

November 4:
THE ROYAL VARIETY SHOW

The Beatles hesitate before playing in front of the Queen Mother during this annual show for the establishment. They end up playing and Lennon, tense, precedes 'Twist And Shout' by saying: "For the people in the cheaper seats clap your hands, and the rest of you if you just rattle your jewellery."

THE BEATLES
I want to hold your hand / This boy

Single/November 63/Parlophone

An ingenuous hit composed by John and Paul in Wimpole Street on Mrs Asher's piano, convincing enough for Capitol in America to finally sign the band and launch them there in 1964.

Its B-side, a slow number reminiscent of 'To Know Him Is To Love Him' by Phil Spector's Teddy Bears, as well as Smokey Robinson, is equally successful.

Fourth number one in a row.
One million copies pre-ordered!

BEATLEMANIA !

The term "Beatlemania" is coined by journalist Sandy Gardiner in November 1963. The English fan club has around 80,000 members at this point. A Sunday Times critic calls Lennon & McCartney the "greatest composers since Beethoven"!

64

After a warm-up concert at the Cyrano in Versailles, our four friends play for three weeks at the Olympia in Paris. The reception is lukewarm at first, but they end up as the stars of a show that also features Trini Lopez, Sylvie Vartan and the very young Pierre Vassiliu. In Paris, The Beatles can hear themselves play without having to endure non-stop screaming by fans. It's bizarre... the calm before the storm?

☐ FROM ME TO YOU ☐☐☐☐ ASK ME WHY ☐☐☐
☐ I SAW HER STANDING THERE ☐ PLEASE PLEASE ME

The Beatles stay in a suite at the Hotel George V. There they compose, discover Bob Dylan's *Freewheelin*, and become bored...

AT THE GEORGE V, GEORGE MARTIN HEARS PAUL PLAYING A NEW SONG ON THE PIANO WHICH HE CALLS 'SCRAMBLED EGGS'.

Sie Liebt Dich
(Yeah, yeah, yeah!)

Sessions at the Pathé-Marconi studios in Boulogne. The Beatles record (dragging their feet) German versions of two of their hits and a new song, 'Can't Buy Me Love'.

FEBRUARY 3
3,000 FANS WELCOME THEM AT KENNEDY AIRPORT.

AT THE CENTRE OF A STORM, THE BEATLES ARE ESCORTED EVERYWHERE BY POLICE CARS. A CROWD OF FANS WAIT FOR THEM OUTSIDE THEIR NEW YORK HOTEL, THE PLAZA. ON AMERICAN RADIO, YOU CAN HEAR A BEATLES SONG EVERY FOUR MINUTES.

I ♡ YOU BEATLES

ED SULLIVAN SHOW

ON FEBRUARY 9, 73 MILLION TELEVISION VIEWERS DISCOVER THE BEATLES FOR THE FIRST TIME. THE NEXT DAY, THOUSANDS OF TEENAGERS FORM BANDS IN THEIR PARENTS' GARAGES AND FORGET TO GO TO THE BARBER.

IT IS ESTIMATED THAT THE CRIME RATE IN THE USA DROPPED BY 15% DURING THE BROADCAST.

TRIUMPHANT MINI-TOUR IN THE USA. AFTER NEW YORK, WASHINGTON IN THE SNOW. IN MIAMI, CONCERTS, TV, PROMO, A DIP IN THE SEA... ... AND A COMIC PHOTO SESSION WITH CASSIUS CLAY.

19 FEV.
WOW! the Beatles are here!
the only AUTHENTIC BEATLE WIG
FITS ALL HEADS SIZE
MADE IN USA

HALF A TON OF WIGS ARE MANUFACTURED IN THE USA.

DURING A COCKTAIL PARTY AT THE BRITISH EMBASSY IN WASHINGTON DC, A GUEST CUTS OFF A LOCK OF RINGO'S HAIR. ANGRY AT THE WAY THEY ARE TREATED, THE BEATLES DECIDE TO BOYCOTT SUCH PARTIES.

SINCE JOINING THE BAND, RINGO HAS BEEN FEELING ISOLATED, NOT QUITE ON THE SAME LEVEL AS JOHN, PAUL & GEORGE...

BUT THE UNITED STATES MAKES

RINGO

A FULL BEATLE.

WITH HIS IMMEDIATELY RECOGNISABLE FACE AND FUNNY NAME, HE BECOMES THE MOST FAMOUS MEMBER OF THE BAND.

FEBRUARY 12 CARNEGIE HALL, NYC.

• TRIBUTES, RIP-OFFS & BEATLEMANIA ODDITIES MADE IN USA, 1964 •

BEATLEMOVIE!!!

BACK FROM THE USA, THE FAB FOUR SHOOT THEIR FIRST FILM FOR UNITED ARTISTS. IT'S AN EXCITING COMEDY IN BLACK AND WHITE ABOUT ONE DAY IN THE LIFE OF THE GROUP AMID THE CHAOS OF BEATLEMANIA. THE DIALOGUE IS INSPIRED BY THE OFF-THE-CUFF HUMOUR OF OUR YOUNG FRIENDS. THE FILM, SHOT BY RICHARD LESTER, IS PEPPERED WITH NEW SONGS THAT WILL CONSTITUTE THE BULK OF THE NEXT ALBUM.

FOR HIS 21ST BIRTHDAY, GEORGE RECEIVES 60 POSTBAGS OF FAN MAIL AND PRESENTS.

In His Own Write

is the title of a collection of "nonsense" poems written by John Lennon and inspired by Lewis Carroll.

The book sells hundreds of thousands of copies on both sides of the Atlantic.

From then on the singer/guitarist is called the "intellectual Beatle".

The famous Madame Tussaud's Museum inaugurates, in the presence of the originals, wax models representing them. They look more or less the same.

On March 19, Government opposition leader Harold Wilson presents the Beatles with a Silver Heart plaque for 'Show Business Personalities of 1963'. John thanks him for the "purple hearts" (the favourite amphetamines of the Mods).

Ringo depressed!

Hospitalised with pharyngitis, he has to be replaced at the last minute for the start of a new tour!

300,000 FANS CHEER THE BEATLES ON THE BALCONY OF THEIR HOTEL IN ADELAIDE, AUSTRALIA.
SUCH A GATHERING MUST EVOKE NUREMBERG IN 1936 FOR JOHN AND PAUL WHO RESPOND TO THE CROWD WITH A HITLER SALUTE.

BEATLE FOR A WEEK!

JIMMY NICOL REPLACES RINGO IN THE MIDDLE OF BEATLEMANIA. DURING REHEARSALS, STRESSED OUT, HE IS OFTEN HEARD SAYING:

"IT'S GETTING BETTER? IT'S GETTING BETTER?"

NEVER SEEN!

On the April 6, the Beatles occupy the first five positions in Billboard singles charts in the USA!

1. CAN'T BUY ME LOVE
2. TWIST AND SHOUT
3. SHE LOVES YOU
4. I WANT TO HOLD YOUR HAND
5. PLEASE PLEASE ME

as well as seven other places in the top 100...

THE BEATLES
Long tall Sally

EP/June 64/Parlophone

An excellent four titles of pure rock'n'roll based on energetic covers of Little Richard, Carl Perkins and Larry Williams... plus one composition by John, the delicious and swaying 'I Call Your Name'.

'Long Tall Sally' has been part of the "wild" repertoire of the band since Hamburg. Paul sings it perfectly, which means he screams like a demented monkey.

BEATSCELLANEOUS

"What do you call your hairstyle?" "Arthur," replies George. A few weeks later a nightclub bearing the name Arthur opened in New York.

In Weybridge (25 miles from London), John settles down with his wife and child in a big house called Kenwood.

Paul offers Drake's Drum, a race horse, to his father, Jim, for his 62nd birthday.

Nicknames:
• The Mop Tops
• 4 Groovy Guys
• The Fab Four
• The 4 From Liverpool

FIVE ENGLISH BANDS RUSH INTO THE BEATLES SLIPSTREAM AND ENJOY SUCCESS IN THE USA:

THE ANIMALS!
GERRY & THE PACEMAKERS!
THE KINKS!
THE ROLLING STONES!
MANFRED MANN!

THE BEATLES
A hard day's night

LP/July 64/Parlophone

The album of Beatlemania, their first recorded on four tracks. Full to the brim with hits.

It's acknowledged that its title, also the name of the film, was coined by Ringo Starr, now noted for his quirky, genial turn of phrase. John is charged with composing a song around the title – it took him 20 minutes. And it's amazing, right from the sensational intro to the last chimes of George Harrison's new 12-string Rickenbacker guitar.

A Hard Day's Night is the first 100% Lennon/McCartney album.

With a much-inspired John Lennon (10 songs out of 13, all finished with Paul), despite indications to the contrary, several of these joyful and energetic songs are about the difficulties faced by John & Cynthia… Paul, although a fan of Little Richard, seems to have discovered a taste for sophisticated ballads, like 'And I Love Her', inspired by Jane Asher.

The usual colossal sales occur almost everywhere.

In Canada, Ringo receives death threats for being an "English Jew".

On stage, to protect himself, he places his cymbals vertically and a policeman stands in front of him.

For the record, Ringo is in no way Jewish!

STEREOTYPES
INHERITED FROM THE FILM
A HARD DAY'S NIGHT.

1. THE INTELLECTUAL
2. THE CHARMER
3. THE PHLEGMATIC
4. THE COMIC

August-September: second monster tour of the USA.

In a hotel where they are staying, a woman is murdered. Her screams blend with those of the fans…

DELMONICO !

IN THEIR NEW YORK HOTEL DYLAN INITIATES THE BEATLES (AND BRIAN EPSTEIN) INTO MARIJUANA. THEY RATHER LIKE IT AND QUICKLY BECOME 'SMOKERS'. APPARENTLY DYLAN IS LOUSY AT ROLLING.

How did you find America?
John: Turn left at Greenland.
Don't you ever get a haircut?
George: Yes, I had one yesterday.
Ringo, why do you wear two rings on each hand?
Ringo: Because I can't fit them through my nose.
Will you sing something for us?
Ringo: No, we need money first.
Which of you is really bald?
George: We're all bald. And I'm deaf and dumb.

PRESS
CONFERENCE

I FEEL FINE
SHE'S A WOMAN

THE BEATLES

𝄞 𝄞 𝄞 𝄞 𝄞 + 𝄞 !

THE BEATLES
I feel fine / She's a woman

Single/October 64/Parlophone

The Beatles are the best team of pop melodists in the kingdom. OK. But on the noise level, the competition is fierce with new bands, the Kinks and Stones at the forefront. With the first ever recorded feedback as an intro and the insistent riff around which 'I Feel Fine' is built, Lennon puts his band back at the top in every compartment of the game.

The B-side, Paul's 'She's A Woman' features chords played in counter time by John to give it a slightly Jamaican feel.

AUGUST-OCTOBER 1964 SESSIONS

Three months after finishing the recording of A Hard Day's Night, they go back to the studio to record a new album planned for December!

The relationship between George Martin and the Beatles evolves.

He is now there to help them, at their request, but no longer to manage the sessions. It seems a long time since he chose their songs!

Recorded but rejected: 'Leave My Kitten Alone'.

Alfred Lennon

Not wishing to cash in on his son's success, of course, John's father reappears. Reluctant to see him again, John finally agrees to talk to him for 20 minutes in Brian Epstein's office. But Alfred gives interview after interview in which he complains that his famous son has abandoned him.

John ends up paying him a kind of alimony.

🅟🅟🅟🅟🅟

THE BEATLES
Beatles for sale

LP/December 64/Parlophone

The heroes are exhausted and it is visible on the sleeve.

After such a year, who wouldn't be! With insufficient time to compose, they dig into covers (of good old fifties rock'n'roll), and old stuff ('I'll Follow The Sun', which Paul composed… in 1958!).

The album's structure is reminiscent of their first album, but although the new songs have been "forced" (ie, composed urgently for the album) they are mostly good and convey the band's evolution.

Indeed, John is influenced by Dylan from now onwards, especially on 'I'm A Loser', on which he displays a more personal and introspective style.

This temporary fatigue gives a more melancholy and occasionally very moving tone to a record that still offers euphoric moments similar to those of *A Hard Day's Night*.

And, damn it, 'Every Little Thing' is bloody excellent.

A Cellarfull Of Noise is the title of Brian Epstein's memoirs (written with Derek Taylor). A book Lennon immediately rechristened: *A Cellarful Of Boys!*

A CELLARFUL OF NOISE

BRIAN EPSTEIN

FOR THE SECOND CONSECUTIVE YEAR, THE BEATLES OFFER THE MEMBERS OF THEIR FAN CLUB A FLEXI-DISC ON WHICH THEY PRESENT BEST WISHES IN THEIR VERY OWN LAIDBACK WAY AND MASSACRE A FEW CHRISTMAS CAROLS.

Very red Englishmen!

In May, George and John take the
sun in Tahiti, on a sailing boat. But
a leopard can't change its spots,
John quickly gets bored...

65

WEDDING + GROOMING

On the February 11 Ringo marries Maureen Cox, 19, hairdresser from Liverpool. They spend their honeymoon in Brighton. "Two down, two to go," George Harrison remarked.

Creation of the Cynthia Lennon fan club.

Here we see John & Cynthia in the park at Kenwood, their home in Weybridge. They and little Julian live in two rooms because the house is being renovated… for nine months now.

USUALLY IT STARTS WITH A PHONE CALL FROM GEORGE MARTIN: "BOYS, WE ARE RECORDING THE NEW ALBUM IN THREE WEEKS TIME."

NO NEED TO PANIC: PAUL, WHO HAS PASSED HIS DRIVING TEST, MEETS UP WITH JOHN AT HIS HOME IN KENWOOD TO COMPLETE THE SONGS THAT EACH HAS COMPOSED INDIVIDUALLY.

• FEBRUARY 1965 SESSIONS:
songs for the second film.

Messing about with the working hours of the venerable EMI, the Beatles start to record in the evening. That way they have the studios to themselves. This comes at the right time because new techniques of overdubbing and double-tracking turn them into studio perfectionists.

INNOVATION: George uses his weird new pedal with "wah-wah" effects on 'I Need You'.
Rejected: 'If You've Got Troubles', 'That Means A Lot'.

TO AVOID THE FANS WAITING FOR HIM OUTSIDE JANE ASHER'S HOUSE, PAUL GOES OVER THE ROOFS, THEN THROUGH A NEIGHBOUR'S WINDOW.

Peter Sellers rejoins his old accomplice, George Martin, to record a Shakespearean version of 'A Hard Day's Night'.

February: the second Beatles film, provisionally called

EIGHT ARMS TO HOLD YOU

is shot in the Bahamas, in colour, though one barely notices. They work with the actress Eleanor Bron, whose first name interests Paul…

…The shoot continues in the Austrian Alps, because the Fab Four want to discover skiing. Smoking marijuana straight after breakfast, our friends lose interest in the project completely, and are permanently doubled up with laughter and incapable of remembering their lines.

LSD

DURING A PARTY, JOHN RILEY, A LONDON DENTIST, SLYLY SLIPS LSD INTO JOHN AND GEORGE'S COFFEES. THAT NIGHT BOTH FEEL "IN LOVE WITH EVERYTHING", AND CONTINUE HALLUCINATING AT THE AD LIB CLUB, WHOSE LIFT APPEARS TO BE ON FIRE!

CLEVER SLEEVE, AT THE TIME WHEN NORTHERN SONGS JOINS THE STOCK MARKET! BEATLES SONGS IN THE CITY!

BEATLES TICKET TO RIDE / YES IT IS

THE BEATLES
Ticket to ride / Yes it is

Single/April 65/Parlophone

'Ticket To Ride' is all about rhythm. Melancholy, yet powerful and rather jerky, John Lennon's song has an atypical tempo that Paul has to explain to Ringo, who is slightly out of his depth.

In Hamburg, a "ticket to ride" was the compulsory work licence for prostitutes.

Very proud of the A-side, Lennon openly detests 'Yes It Is', a slow number in the manner of 'This Boy', dating from 1963, a century ago in the Beatle calendar.

DISILLUSIONED

John Lennon cries for help. Disillusioned by fame, unhappy in his marriage, he puts on weight and plunges into cynicism and melancholia. The psychotropic drugs he takes help him cultivate his paranoia. In the film *Help!*, he appears elsewhere, as if the Beatles already weigh heavily on him…

🎸🎸🎸🎸🎸 + 🎸 !

THE BEATLES
Help! / I'm down

Single/ July 65/ Parlophone

John Lennon has followed Bob Dylan's advice: he must write his songs with the same care he brings to writing his books.

No more songs like 'She Loves You'. Lennon writes songs from the heart, and is unable to compromise.

'Help!' gives its name to the film and becomes an instant classic.

For the B-side, Paul succeeds in composing an excellent song influenced by Little Richard.

THANK YOU LUCKY STAR !

In the space of one year, the Fab Four are seen 11 times on British television!

Their signs mean N-U-J-V in semaphore.

JIMMY NICOL, THE DRUMMER WHO REPLACED RINGO FOR A WEEK DURING THE AUSTRALIAN TOUR IN 1964, DECLARES HIMSELF BANKRUPT.

Cut Piece

At Carnegie Hall, a happening by the Fluxus artist YOKO ONO. The audience is invited to cut off her clothes with a pair of scissors.

She ends up naked.

THE BEATLES mono
HELP!

While John is entering a period of self-doubt, Paul swims like a fish through the ocean of Swinging London. His old song 'Scrambled Eggs' has become 'Yesterday', a true classic, not even released as a single in the UK!

After Lennon, McCartney finds his own path amongst the mutating Beatles.

DELIGHTED!

THE BEATLES
Help!

LP/August 65/Parlophone

Structured around three huge hits, 'Help!', 'Ticket To Ride' and 'Yesterday', this fifth LP confirms Dylan's influence ("folk-rock" has been used recently), without losing The Beatles' magic touch, the one that transforms lead into a gold record.

Looser than the previous albums, the songs on *Help!* gain in scope, and the influence of country music makes their universe evolve still more.

'Yesterday' definitely places The Beatles in the pantheon of great songwriters, though it bothers its composers to some degree. Composed and interpreted by Paul alone, with a string quartet as sole accompaniment, Lennon refuses to let the album finish on this note, and screams an old rock number from Hamburg, 'Dizzy Miss Lizzie', as the last track.

Pure jealousy? Though 'Yesterday' might appear rather syrupy, 'Dizzy' is slightly laboured, and its presence is only justified by the sheer will to sabotage the previous song.

ROCK'N'ROLL ATTITUDE!

SHEA STADIUM!
15/08/65

THE BIGGEST CONCERT OF ALL TIME: 56,000 SPECTATORS! THE BEATLES, IN THEIR FINE BEIGE JACKETS WITH MAO COLLARS, ARRIVE BY HELICOPTER AND TAKE TO A STAGE NOT MUCH BIGGER THAN THE ONE AT THE CAVERN CLUB. LENNON, GONE MAD, PLAYS THE ORGAN WITH HIS ELBOWS WHILE SINGING GOD KNOWS WHAT. ANYWAY, NOBODY SEES ANYTHING OR HEARS ANYTHING EVEN THOUGH VOX HAD CREATED 100-WATT SPEAKERS SPECIALLY FOR THEM!

You like The Beatles? You might like:

Second attempt at recording a Beatles concert at the Hollywood Bowl for a hypothetical live album.

Only the screams of the fans can be heard.

JUDAS!

Dylan offered them marijuana, the Beatles show him the way to electricity. But the folk purists don't see it that way...

Politically incorrect

Regularly, before a concert, our four friends are obliged to meet handicapped children who have come to see their idols, and it terrorizes John Lennon who, as a release, imitates them on stage.

August 20

During a party in LA organised by The Byrds (the band that makes Dylan sound like he's from Liverpool), actor Peter Fonda, on acid, keeps repeating: "I know what it's like to be dead." Lennon asks Mal Evans to write it down for later...

Bel Air 27/08/65 11p.m.

The Beatles arrive at the home of Elvis, the hero of their youth. The meeting is pretty sterile. They talk, play some music (the King is learning the bass). Nothing more.

On leaving, John admits disappointment. The rebel from 1956 is now a blasé actor of Hollywood tripe.

The AMERICAN discography

Though the quartet makes it a point of honour to control their British releases, this proves impossible in other countries. Each label does what they want, if not absolutely anything and everything. In America, different sleeves and albums titles are released. Above all, the Capitol albums have 11 songs instead of the 14 in Britain! And the unreleased singles are included! So the American kids have six albums by their favourite band while the British only have five!

September:
birth of Zak Starkey.
"I won't let Zak be a drummer," declares dad Ringo.

WHISKY VERSUS MARIJUANA

The old generation retaliates! During a television show, Dean Martin sings: "I hate the Beatles!"

IS IT ME OR DOES IT SOUND QUITE SIMILAR?

'If I Needed Someone' and 'Bells Of Rhymney' by The Byrds.

●

'Ticket To Ride' and 'Girl, Don't Tell Me' by the Beach Boys.

THE BEATLES IN A CARTOON
ON AMERICAN TELEVISION!
THE GRAPHIC BIBLE IS CREATED
BY PETER SANDER.

October-November: sessions for album two of 1965.

With only four weeks to record and not enough material, they have to write urgently once again. Those who attend the sessions talk about an ambience more folksy, more introspective than for Help!.

One day, Brian Epstein bursts unannounced into the studio to give his opinion of the music he hears. John gives vent to his anger: "We'll make the records. You just go on counting your percentages."

sitar !

The strange "gling gling" heard on 'Norwegian Wood' is a sitar, George's new passion. He had discovered the Indian instrument during the shooting of *Help!* and bought himself one in India Craft.

However, the Kinks' 'See My Friends', released in July, is the first pop song to feature that instrument.

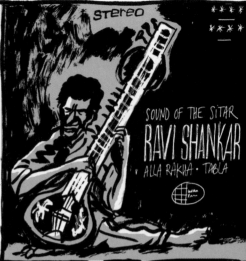

STEREO

SOUND OF THE SITAR
RAVI SHANKAR
ALLA RAKHA · TABLA

THE BEATLES
WE CAN WORK IT OUT
DAY TRIPPER

A 5389

The music of Lennon & McCartney

A TV SHOW BROADCAST ON GRANADA PRESENTS JOHN AND PAUL. THEIR GUESTS: THE GEORGE MARTIN ORCHESTRA, MARIANNE FAITHFUL, PETER & GORDON AND... DICK RIVERS!

India Craft Ltd
The Treasure house of Indian Handcrafts
51 OXFORD STREET, LONDON, W.1
GERrard 1479
254, KENSINGTON HIGH STREET, LONDON, W.8
WEStern 2814

MBE

On October 16, the Beatles receive MBEs. It is controversial. Old military men, shocked, send theirs back. They smoke cigarettes in the toilets at Buckingham Palace and the Queen, pinning on their decorations, asks how long they've been together. "Forty years," replies Ringo.

Many (him included) think that Brian Epstein also deserves the honour.

**THE BEATLES
We can work it out / Day tripper**

Single/December 65/Parlophone

'We Can Work It Out', by Paul, has everything to make an excellent A-side, but John absolutely wants it to be his 'Day Tripper' whose riff was pure Rolling Stones (it's the year of 'Satisfaction'). So EMI invents for its darling Beatles the DOUBLE A-SIDE! These two superb songs, which skirt around sex, drugs and Paul's shaky relationship with Jane Asher, are an undeniable summit of Sixties rock.

♫♫♫♫♫+♫ !

THE BEATLES
Rubber soul

LP/December 65/Parlophone

The beginning of their fabulous mid-period. "We finally took over the studio," said Lennon.

Some fans are horrified to discover a sleeve without the band's name (daring), showing a distorted photo of the Fab Four with sick eyes and the fixed grins of dope smokers.

Dope increased their ambition. Feeling inferior to Dylan's aura, they sense it's the moment to move on to the next stage of their development, no longer the rather juvenile clowns in the Help! film. Primarily, this album is not a succession of singles with a few covers as fillers. The album is considered as a whole, a kind of musical piece lasting 36 minutes, composed of songs of 2.30. John's songs ('Norwegian Wood', 'Nowhere Man', 'Girl' and the autobiographical 'In My Life') are more personal and Paul's bass is increasingly melodic and punchy.

Warm and melancholic like a fire on a Sunday evening, it is the autumnal album par excellence, as well as all the other seasons since 1965.

BEEP, BEEP, BEEP BEEP, YEAAAAH!

TOP OF THE POPS
!!

November 25:
the prestigious
London department store
Harrods
closes its doors
so that the Beatles
can do their
Christmas shopping.

THAT'S MY LIFE

IS THE TITLE OF THE SINGLE BY THAT OLD CROOK FREDDIE LENNON, REMARRIED TO ONE OF HIS SON'S YOUNG FANS.

PYE

?THE WORD IS...

LOVE. YES, BUT THAT LOVE IS NOT THE LOVE OF SENTIMENTAL SONGS LIKE 'FROM ME TO YOU'... IN SAN FRANCISCO, THOSE WHO ARE NOW CALLED "HIPPIES" BEGIN TO LET FLOWERS GROW IN THEIR HAIR.

In the CHRISTMAS RECORD for this year, our friends massacre 'Yesterday', pastiche Dylan and sing a carol!

HAPPY CHRISTMAS Beatle People !

"COPYRRRIGHT JOHNNY!"

" LORDS

One evening as Paul was having a drink at a friend's house, a policeman rang the doorbell to ask for an Aston Martin to be moved as it was badly parked on the pavement. Paul appeared at the door. "Oh, it's you, sir. If you don't mind giving me the keys, I'll park it properly and bring them back," he said.

PAUL,

the only one living in London, is like a sponge. He goes out a lot and meets people in the world of culture (like the gallery owner Robert Fraser) who initiate him into the avant-garde.

John, who feels stuck in Kenwood, has an inferiority complex vis-à-vis Paul.

INDICA
102 Southampton Row

The pop art gallery run by John Dunbar and Barry Miles opens its bookshop. The first customer is Paul McCartney, their friend and benefactor, who has created the design for the flyers and bags.

Paul, who wants to know if he could be successful without the label Lennon/McCartney, writes a song for Peter & Gordon under the pseudonym Bernard Webb. It goes to 14 in the USA and 28 in England.

George + Pattie

GEORGE HARRISON MARRIES THE MODEL PATTIE BOYD, WHOM HE HAD MET ON THE SHOOT OF *A HARD DAY'S NIGHT*. SHE IS ONE OF THE SCHOOLGIRLS IN THE TRAIN SCENES.

PAUL IS THE WITNESS.

THE PSYCHEDELIC EXPERIENCE

A MANUAL BASED ON THE TIBETAN BOOK OF THE DEAD

BY
TIMOTHY LEARY, Ph.D
RALPH METZNER, Ph.D
RICHARD ALPERT, Ph.D

TURN OFF YOUR MIND, RELAX AND FLOAT DOWN STREAM

.... is the first sentence in a book written by the LSD pope, Timothy Leary, based on the Tibetan Book of the Dead.

John Lennon has bought it at Indica and he is now initiated in psychedelia (hallucinations due to the ingestion of acid).

He uses the sentence in his song 'Tomorrow Never Knows'.

Sessions album 66

(April/June)

The watchword seems to be: EXPERIMENTATION. The first song recorded, titled 'Mark 1' or 'The Void', sets the tone. A super powerful electronic mantra with John's voice sounding "like a Dalai Lama singing on a hilltop".

Revolutionary!

Geoff Emerick,

aged 19, becomes the Beatles' sound engineer. He gives them added power and helps them find solutions for their inventiveness by breaking the strict and outdated rules at EMI's studios.

Yellow Submarine !

MARIANNE FAITHFUL AND BRIAN JONES TAKE PART IN THE RECORDING OF THIS AMUSING CHILDREN'S SONG SUNG BY RINGO. AMIDST THE PARTY ATMOSPHERE, LIKE A TRENDY FANFARE UNDER THE INFLUENCE OF ALCOHOL, EVERYONE ENDS UP DOING A CONGA, FOLLOWING MAL EVANS, WHO CARRIES A BIG DRUM ON HIS CHEST.

THE DIRECTOR OF THE STUDIOS HAPPENS TO WITNESS THE SCENE, THOUGH HE DIDN'T ATTEND THE EVENING SESSIONS.

IN LOVING MEMORY OF

MY DEAR HUSBAND
JOHN RIGBY
WHO DEPARTED THIS LIFE
OCT 4TH 1916 AGED 72 YEARS
"AT REST"
ALSO FRANCES WIFE OF THE ABOVE
DIED APRIL 3RD 1922 AGED 85 YEARS
ALSO DORIS W. DAUGHTER OF
ERIE RIGBY DIED DEC 24TH 1922
AGED 2 YEARS N 3 MONTHS
ALSO

ELEANOR RIGBY

THE BELOVED WIFE OF THOMAS WOODS
AND GRANDDAUGHTER OF THE ABOVE
DIED 4TH OCT 1939 AGED 44 YEARS
ASLEEP
ALSO FRANCES
DAUGHTER OF THE ABOVE
DIED 2ND NOVEMBER 1949
AGED 71 YEARS

Chiswick House

May 1966
Promotional videos are shot in this West London public gardens, for 'Paperback Writer' and 'Rain'.

Paul is recovering from a bicycle fall which has cost him an incisor tooth. It gives him a nasty medieval smile.

PAPERBACK WRITER c/w RAIN

🎸🎸🎸🎸🎸 + 🎸 !

THE BEATLES
Paperback writer / Rain

Single/June 66/Parlophone

- -

For the first time on a Beatles record, the bass is the motor of the new songs. That's because, for the first time since 1962, ONE CAN HEAR THE BASS! It's the considerable contribution of Geoff Emerick to the Beatles sound.
Paul had heard rhythm'n'blues in clubs for years with enormous bass sounds and didn't understand why the instrument was under-mixed on English pop records.

'Paperback Writer' by Paul is both aggressive and soft, with the French nursery rhyme 'Frère Jacques' harmonised by John and George in the background.

'Rain', the B-side, is pure 1966 psychedelic Lennon. A hallucinogenic and oriental-style ballad, strangely cotton wool-like, as if in slow motion. In the end John's voice is recorded backwards, experimenting with tapes being our friends' new hobby.

It's also the favourite single of the author of this book.

The Beach Boys Pet Sounds

Capitol

You like The Beatles? You might also like:

Pet Sounds by the Beach Boys is the album of the year for Paul, who is fond of those complex melodies and the ultra-slick production. And deservedly so too, for Brian Wilson has thrown himself into that record after listening to Rubber Soul. Shaken by the Beatles album, he embarked on the creation of a very personal work on which no member of his band played a single note...

SHE SAID SHE SAID

For the first time, the Fab Four assist at the mix of the new album. But George Martin realises it is one song short! John, who loves a challenge, improvises and records a final track in nine hours!

Paul has bought a farm in West Scotland, far away from the horrors of Beatlemania.

This garage-rock band based in Germany wants to look mean, dirty and nasty. Their monkish tonsure makes anti-Beatles of these ex-GIs.

!!! Shocking !!!

Paul insists that this photo, taken by Robert Whitaker of our friends dressed up as butchers amongst mutilated dolls and pieces of meat, be used for the sleeve of this American compilation. The image was supposed to express the Beatles' point of view on the Vietnam War.

Not surprisingly, record shops in the US refuse to stock it. 750,000 copies are sent back and it is decided to stick a more anodyne picture on top of the first.

The fans lose no time steaming off the new photo to discover what caused all the fuss!

The Beatles Yesterday And Today

← A collector's item to kill for!

The Indian sitar player Ravi Shankar, a living legend, gives an exceptional concert in London.

George Harrison welcomes his new hero warmly at Heathrow Airport, dressed in traditional Indian clothes.

As for Shankar, he descends from the plane in an impeccable suit made in England.

Les Beatles de 40
l'assassin • la rose noire
un jour tu verras
mouloudji

disques mouloudji
festival

The Beatles return to Hamburg for a German mini-tour. They meet up with their friend Astrid Kirchherr who gives John the letters he had written to Stu from 1961 to '62.

Very touched, Lennon says it was the most beautiful present he has ever received.

KLAUS HUMANN:

BRAVO - BEATLES BLITZ TOUR 1966!

"IT WAS A SUNDAY, THE SUNDAY JUNE 26, 1966. TWO TICKETS FOR THE BEATLES CONCERT IN HAMBURG, BUT THE CONDITION MY PARENTS HAD IMPOSED ON THEIR 16-YEAR-OLD SON WAS THAT MY MOTHER ACCOMPANY ME. IMAGINE THE SHAME.

"AFTER THREE MINUTES, ALL WAS FORGOTTEN. THAT ROTTEN CONCRETE HALL, THE SHABBY FOLDING CHAIRS, THE THOUSANDS OF MAD FANS AROUND US, MY MOTHER, EVERYTHING.

"WHILE SHE COVERED HER EARS, I WAS STANDING ON MY CHAIR WAVING MY CARDIGAN LIKE CRAZY. WE COULDN'T UNDERSTAND A WORD OF THE LYRICS FOR WE WERE TOO NOISY AND THE ACOUSTICS WERE RUBBISH. BUT WE SAVOURED EACH OF THOSE 30 MINUTES OF THAT SHORT BEATLES SET.

"THE OTHER BANDS, IF I REMEMBER WELL, WERE PETER & GORDON, THE GIRL GROUP THE LIVERBIRDS AND OUR BEST LOCAL BAND, THE RATTLES.
"IT WAS THE GIG OF MY LIFE EVEN THOUGH I DON'T REMEMBER IT MUCH. ONLY THAT ELECTRIC SHIVER DOWN MY SPINE FOR THE FIRST TIME. THAT SUNDAY, I BECAME A ROCK FAN."

TODAY KLAUS IS THE BOSS OF CARLSEN VERLAG.

BUDOKAN BLUES

July: concerts in Japan. In that mythical hall dedicated to sumo, there is one policeman for every two spectators.

The result is that the audience maintain a religious silence. It is a reality check for our friends who suddenly become aware of the mediocrity of their performance which is usually concealed by the fans' pandemonium.

All the more so for the sophisticated new songs, which are very difficult to play live.

THE CURSED TOUR

The concerts in the Philippines are a resounding success. Nearly 100,000 spectators cheer our friends. But, having declined an invitation to attend a cocktail reception in their honour, the Beatles throw the dictator president's wife, Imelda Marcos, into a rage.

They are pushed around, threatened and chased unceremoniously at the airport. The plane remains firmly on the ground. Brian Epstein is ordered to disembark. There's total panic. The gentle giant Mal Evans bursts into tears.

After the manager has been stripped of the takings from the concerts, the plane is finally allowed to depart...

Klaus Voormann, their old friend from Hamburg, is the creator of the new album's sleeve.

"BEATLES MORE POPULAR THAN CHRIST."

Taken out of context, this extract from an interview given by John Lennon to Maureen Cleave a few months earlier is used as a pretext by American extremists to stoke up their prejudice against the Beatles and all they represent. The scandal is such that Epstein wants to cancel the US tour which is being prepared.

The Fab Four refuse.

Beatles trash

In the Southern States, several bonfires of Beatles records are organised.

The Klu Klux Klan threatens to kill the band.

John Lennon gives a press conference to explain himself. But he refuses to apologise.

Paul was seen at the beginning of the year attending a concert by the electronic composer Berio.

The Beatles have since bought themselves recording equipment to play around with at home. It's a competition as to who will produce the most astonishing sounds.

As for John, he is particularly fond of backwards tapes and other bizarre and random sounds.

⚜⚜⚜⚜⚜ + ⚜ !

THE BEATLES
Revolver

LP/August 66/Parlophone

A kaleidoscopic masterpiece with: saturation – satire – cowbell – riff – ruffled solo – Ah ah Mr Wilson – Look at all the lonely people – Baroque & heart-rending – Stay in bed – float up stream – backwards tapes – soft ballad – Ragga rock – Bollywood finale – heavenly harmonies – Ringo – fanfare – nursery rhymes – drinking song – sound effects – And the band begins to play – When I was a boy, everything was right – psychedelia – piercing noise – I feel good in a very special way – jazzy solo – binary – majestic bridge – funky bass – French horn solo – bitterness – arm hair standing on end – Well well well you are feeling fine – acid – I could wait forever I've got time – Rhythm'n'blues brass – Stax blaze – groovy Stockhausen & seagulls –

WORKING TITLES FOR REVOLVER:

ABRACADABRA
AFTER GEOGRAPHY
BEATLES ON SAFARI
FAT MAN & BOBBY
FOUR SIDES OF THE ETERNAL TRIANGLE
MAGIC CIRCLE
PENDULUM

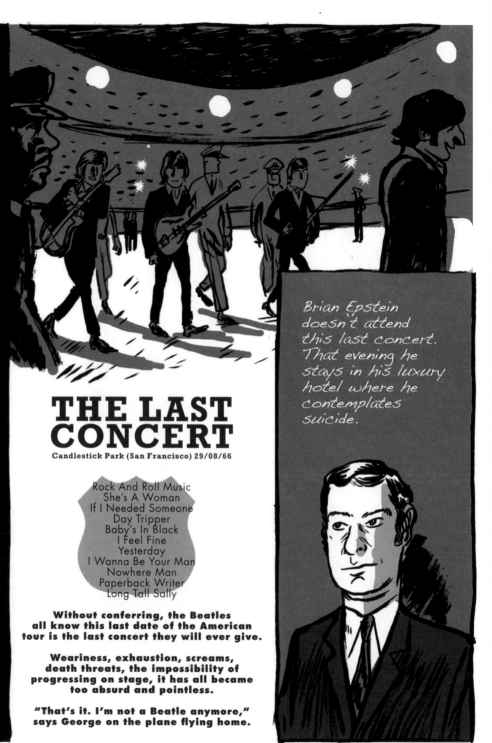

THE LAST CONCERT
Candlestick Park (San Francisco) 29/08/66

Rock And Roll Music
She's A Woman
If I Needed Someone
Day Tripper
Baby's In Black
I Feel Fine
Yesterday
I Wanna Be Your Man
Nowhere Man
Paperback Writer
Long Tall Sally

Without conferring, the Beatles all know this last date of the American tour is the last concert they will ever give.

Weariness, exhaustion, screams, death threats, the impossibility of progressing on stage, it has all became too absurd and pointless.

"That's it. I'm not a Beatle anymore," says George on the plane flying home.

Brian Epstein doesn't attend this last concert. That evening he stays in his luxury hotel where he contemplates suicide.

Paul finances the underground newspaper International Times.

George, without doubt the Beatle most weary of Beatlemania, flies to India. He takes sitar classes with Ravi Shankar, as the master's disciple. But he is seeking something else in India.

The meaning of life, perhaps?

September to November 1966

After the end of a depressing tour, everyone feels the need to take a break. Rumours of the band splitting are flying around.

John leaves for Spain to shoot Richard Lester's film How I Won The War, with him in a lead role.

Photos show him slimmer, with cropped hair. Nowadays he keeps his glasses on. He composes 'Strawberry Fields Forever' in his hotel room.

BEATLE ON SAFARI

In the airplane returning from Africa Paul comes up with the idea for the Sergeant Pepper Orchestra, a new incarnation of the Beatles, who are a bit moribund in their present form.

A new band must arise from the ashes of the Fab Four.

A more experimental band to plunge into 1967 counterculture.

Under the big clock in Bordeaux, Mal Evans meets up with Paul who's wearing a moustache to remain incognito. He has been refused entrance to a Bordeaux nightclub because of it...

They decide to leave for Kenya on a video safari...

Yes.

John Lennon meets Yoko Ono at her exhibition of conceptual art in the Indica gallery.

He climbs a ladder and sees "Yes" written on the ceiling, in very small letters.

He likes it a lot.

A pretty dull compilation except for the inclusion of the rocking 'Bad Boy', until now unavailable in Europe.

"Not only... But also"

John plays the part of Dan the nightclub doorman to an underground men's lavatory in a comedy programme broadcast on the BBC at Christmas.

good vibrations ?

The healthy competition between the Beatles and the Beach Boys continues. While EMI despairs of the lack of a new record by the Fab Four for Xmas, Brian Wilson, galvanized by the audacity of Revolver, throws himself into a fantastic new album, whose big budget single, 'Good Vibrations', is released in advance and meets with a colossal success.

But what are the Beatles up to?

End of December
Although the Beatles have
been in the studio for a
month, a TV crew films them
arriving at Abbey Road. All
wear moustaches, to the
fans' utter amazement.

Have they gone mad?

November 1966

Paul has no trouble persuading the other three of the need for a new challenge to reignite the band.

George Martin doesn't understand what they want to do.

"It's quite simple," Lennon replies, irritated. "We no longer want to play the cute Fab Four. We won't do any more concerts, therefore we can create music that would be impossible to play on stage. We want to make our best album and it might take time."

STRAWBERRY FIELDS FOREVER

For this first song recorded during the sessions, the technicians have to work miracles. They put together two versions at two different tempos and ambiences to satisfy John, its psychedelic creator (here on the Mellotron, that strange organ with tapes, that features in the intro of the song).

Northern *soul*

The first songs recorded for the new album ('Strawberry Fields Forever', 'Penny Lane', 'When I'm 64') indicate the tone and concept: nostalgia for the North of England spirit of their youth (not that distant, the oldest Beatle is 26).

During the long sessions for 'Penny Lane', George Martin brings in the country's best piccolo player, who plays to perfection a quasi-impossible part created by Paul (who can't read music and doesn't want to).

Paul asks the virtuoso if he can do better.

Martin protests: "You cannot ask him that!"

The flute was eventually dropped from the final mix.

...Six to go"

is the working title of the new album, as Brian Epstein has just signed a new contract with EMI agreeing to a further seven albums by the Beatles.

67

Commissioned by the Roundhouse Theatre for a psychedelic evening, Paul records an abstract musical piece lasting 13 minutes and 48 seconds called

'A CARNIVAL OF LIGHT'.

Shooting of the mysterious clip for 'Strawberry...' at Knole Park in Sevenoaks.

The Beatles

Psychedelirium

On the evening of February 10 Paul takes charge of directing an orchestra of 41 musicians playing the noisy orchestral part for the never-ending song 'A Day In The Life'. Prestigious guests attend the event. To make the party complete, the musicians are asked to wear false moustaches and noses. Some refuse, outraged, and leave the studio.

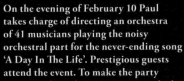

THE BEATLES
Strawberry Fields forever / Penny Lane

Single/February 67/Parlophone

- -

She must have pulled a face, that 14-year-old-fan who placed the needle on this new single from her darling Mop Tops.

In this apocalyptic music, a guy with a moustache and glasses does his own psychoanalysis in a strange voice from beyond the grave...
A lost paradise, Strawberry Fields is of course the garden of the orphanage where John used to play when he was little.

The other A-side, for it is again a double A-side, is on more familiar territory. Paul has synthesized his two passions of the moment, the hyper-clean sound of The Beach Boys and the Bach of the Brandenburg Concerto.
Penny Lane, a street in Liverpool, immediately becomes a cult location for fans.

This single is the first since 'Love Me Do' not to reach number one, remaining stuck in second place.
It is an extraordinary foretaste of what the Beatles are concocting...

This is Engelbert Humperdinck, the old-fashioned crooner who broke the Beatles run of consecutive number ones with 'Please Release Me'.

EMI announce that total sales of Beatles records, all formats taken together, approach

200 million.

On top of that, 446 covers of 'Yesterday' have been recorded.

You like The Beatles? You might also like:

PINK FLOYD

PABLO FANQUES CIRCUS ROYAL

Grandest Night of the Season!

LAST NIGHT BUT THREE!

BEING FOR THE

BENEFIT OF MR. KITE.

MR. J. HENDERSON

THE CELEBRATED SOMERSET THROWER

· PABLO · FANQUES CIRCUS

During the shoot for 'Strawberry', Lennon bought this 1843 poster from an antique dealer. Fascinated, he wrote the song 'Being For The Benefit Of Mr Kite', its lyrics taken from this precious document.

NORMAN SMITH, THE BEATLES EX-SOUND ENGINEER PRESENTS HIS NEW PROTÉGÉS, PINK FLOYD, WHO ARE RECORDING THEIR FIRST ALBUM IN EMI STUDIOS AS WELL.

PINK FLOYD

SYD BARRETT AND ROGER WATERS ARE INTIMIDATED AND PAUL AND GEORGE, THE ONLY TWO BEATLES PRESENT THAT DAY, SEEM TO BE RATHER COLD AND DISTANT.

INFAMOUS SESSIONS

On March 17, Paul, in full creative hyperactivity, cannot wait for George Martin, unavailable for the day, and calls for another producer to arrange the strings for his song 'She's Leaving Home'.

Martin is hurt.

GEORGE

The "third Beatle" seems to have stayed in India, in his mind anyway. His only piece on the album, 'Within You Without You', using no western musical instruments, has left the others wondering… until John declares he likes it. Harrison is finally treated less condescendingly within the band. But, in the studio, they never spend as much time on his compositions as on those by Paul and John….

RINGO

Ringo is often treated as a subordinate, used to obeying orders without offence. With Paul's help, his drumming has become more complex, especially on 'A Day In The Life', in which he proves quite remarkable. During these sessions, he has learned to play chess to stave off his boredom.

BAD TRIP

JOHN LENNON IS THE VICTIM OF A BAD LSD TRIP DURING A RECORDING. GEORGE MARTIN, WHO KNOWS NOTHING ABOUT IT, SUGGESTS HE GETS SOME FRESH AIR ON THE ROOF OF THE STUDIOS (THE ONLY PLACE WITH SOME AIR AND NO HYSTERICAL FANS).

WHEN PAUL IS TOLD, HE RUSHES OUT IN CASE JOHN DECIDES TO TRY TO FLY BY JUMPING OFF.

THEN HE TAKES HIM BACK TO HIS NEARBY HOME, MAKES HIM LIE DOWN AND TAKES SOME ACID HIMSELF TO ACCOMPANY HIS FRIEND ON A LONG TRIPPING NIGHT.

SERGEANT PEPPER AND HIS LONELY HEARTS CLUB BAND

will be photographed with their friends on March 30, 1967 in Flood Street, London. Expected are the gurus, the Beatles from Madame Tussaud, Oscar Wilde, Tony Curtis… Hitler won't make it in the end, to John's great regret.

Michael Cooper takes the photo for the sleeve of Sgt Pepper's, conceived by the pop artist Peter Blake, who has taken two weeks to prepare the decor. He's the little one with the beard, over there.

SMILE?

The day after the mix of Sgt Pepper, Paul flies to Los Angeles. He meets up with a mentally disturbed Brian Wilson who has been working in vain for months on the new Beach Boys album. In the studio with his friend and rival, Paul munches on celery on the song 'Vega-tables', then sits at the piano and plays 'She's Leaving Home' to an astonished Brian. The following week, Wilson sinks into a serious depression and the album Smile is put on hold. It's the end of the battle between the Beatles and Beach Boys.

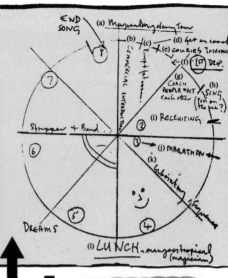

On a plane returning after a trip to the US, Paul draws this pie, the structure of a new project for a film and an album called *MAGICAL MYSTERY TOUR*.

It sounds crazy

but 15 days after the end of the Pepper sessions, the Beatles are already back in the studio!

On the night of the May 9, in an acid haze, they record seven hours of sterile jam without even tuning their instruments.

George Martin leaves before the end in disgust.

During this giant happening in London, the psychedelic crowd spot John Lennon, somewhat bemused, wandering about drugged up to the eyeballs. He leaves just before Pink Floyd's set.

Perpetual Groove!

At the end of the second side there is a brief snatch of psychedelic nonsense which repeats endlessly. Then a 20 hertz whiste that only dogs can hear!

BAG O' NAILS CLUB

*Welcomes members
and their guests...*

❈

*On May 15, Paul meets the
American photographer Linda Eastman
at the Bag O'Nails, a club patronised by pop stars,
where he has a reserved table.*

*Then they go on to the nearby
Speakeasy, where Paul hears '
A Whiter Shade Of Pale', Procol Harum's
baroque masterpiece, for the first time.*

radio

The BBC bans
'A Day In The Life'
because it alludes
to drugs. A pirate
radio station plays
Sgt Pepper
in its entirety
the day before
it is released.

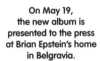

LUCY

*A DRAWING BY
JULIAN LENNON
(AGED 4) DEPICTED
HIS CLASSMATE LUCY
O'DONNELL" IN THE SKY
WITH DIAMONDS".*

On May 19,
the new album is
presented to the press
at Brian Epstein's home
in Belgravia.

A rumour has been
spreading for weeks
that the Beatles
are again going to
make their competitors
look ridiculous.

Paul has shaved off
his moustache.
For him Pepper already
belongs to the past.

**THE BEATLES
Sgt Pepper's lonely hearts club band**

LP/June 67/Parlophone

- -

Relax! Breathe deeply before making
a start on this. Rid yourself of clichés,
conventions and puns.

This album is a masterpiece, alright.
Cornerstone of pop culture bla bla bla.
The four have given birth to a mountain.
Bla bla bla. Moustaches from Zappa
to Carnaby Street. A sitar is born. New
audience, more adult. Huge success.
Street cred on the hippie front. The
album of superlatives. 700 hours in the
studio. The most expensive manifesto-
sleeve of all times. "A splendid time
is guaranteed for all," and the whole
caboodle.

First concept album. But what is
the concept? It is not really British
nostalgia, The Kinks have done that with
their album Something Else. The circus?
Two and a half songs. The East? Drugs?
"These little slugs have turned into
butterflies?"
Maybe.

In reality, an exciting album, at times
magical, but the lack of spontaneity
makes it a tad frosty and intimidating.

There, I said it.

Three days after the release of the album, Hendrix plays the song Sgt Pepper at the Saville Theatre. The Beatles, in the audience, are flattered and delighted.

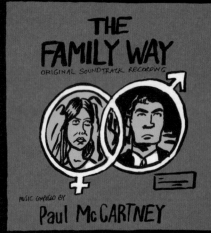

THE FAMILY WAY
ORIGINAL SOUNDTRACK RECORDING

MUSIC COMPOSED BY Paul McCARTNEY

**PAUL McCARTNEY & GEORGE MARTIN
The family way**

LP/June 67/Decca

This is the first solo album by a Beatle, although the involvement of George Martin as arranger is noticeable. Recorded at the end of 1966, the few themes written by Paul are reminiscent of 'Penny Lane' and number a dozen variations with different orchestrations. Nice job. Sentimental, slightly kitsch music. Like the film really.

BRIAN JONES PLAYS THE SAXOPHONE ON THE CRAZY SONG 'YOU KNOW MY NAME (LOOK UP THE NUMBER)' THAT IS DESTINED TO BE THE BEATLES NEXT SINGLE...

June 19: in a television interview at home, Paul admits to taking LSD.

SCANDAL!

Hippie hippie hurrah

On June 25, the Beatles take part in the first global TV broadcast via satellite and sing, partially live, 'All You Need Is Love', composed at top speed for the occasion, in front of 400 million viewers.

John plays the cool dude, chewing gum while singing, but in reality he is dead nervous.

LOVE liebe

John's psychedelic Rolls

THE BEATLES
All you need is love / Baby you're a rich man

Single/July 67/Parlophone

A hymn to universal love both irritating and bloody brilliant. Using samples before they were fashionable, 'La Marseillaise' is the intro and, in the final notes, there's some Glenn Miller as well as a snatch of 'She Loves You', an echo of a bygone era. The B-side is insufferable.

The laziest man in England.

That's the title of an article on John Lennon. It's true that in summer 1967, John spends most of his time lying down, leafing through books and newspapers and experimenting with various substances.

He seldom goes out, doesn't hold any parties at home, even though his house has several reception halls.

JULY

THE BEATLES ARE IN GREECE TO BUY AN ISLAND ON WHICH TO LIVE IN A COMMUNE. AN ODD IDEA — IT'S A COUNTRY WHERE THE MILITARY RULERS FORBID ROCK MUSIC AND LONG HAIR. IN THE END, THE IDEA IS ABANDONED BUT THE HOLIDAY IS WONDERFUL.

Haight Ashbury

August 8: George wanders in the famous hippie area of San Francisco playing the guitar, but he freaks out when faced with filthy junky teenagers who gather around him, and discreetly escapes…

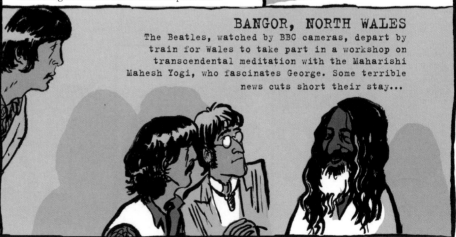

BANGOR, NORTH WALES
The Beatles, watched by BBC cameras, depart by train for Wales to take part in a workshop on transcendental meditation with the Maharishi Mahesh Yogi, who fascinates George. Some terrible news cuts short their stay…

Brian Epstein dies on August 27 of an overdose of sleeping pills.

Suffering from depression since the Beatles stopped touring, he felt his influence diminishing vis-à-vis the band he had taken out of a cellar and pushed to the top of the world in the space of a few years.

Today the Beatles are giant superstars, worshipped by the young as well as by the intellectual elite.

The Epstein family refuse to let the Beatles attend the synagogue so as to preserve the serenity of the funeral service.

MAGICAL MYSTERY TOUR

THE SHOOT PROVES TO BE CHAOTIC AND STRANGE. THERE IS NO REAL SCRIPT OR FILM DIRECTION, IT IS ALL LINK SHOTS.

IT VAGUELY TALKS ABOUT A SIGHTSEEING JOURNEY BY BUS AND IS INTERCUT WITH NEW SONGS.

September 5: crisis meeting at McCartney's Cavendish Avenue home to talk about the future of the band. John, George and Ringo, completely paralysed, leave it to Paul. They decide shooting for the film Magical Mystery Tour should start as soon as possible.

GOO GOO GOO JOOB!

INSPIRED BY "GOOGOO GOOSTH", PAGE 557 IN JAMES JOYCE'S FINNEGANS WAKE, THE SONG 'I AM THE WALRUS' IS THE ONLY MAGIC MOMENT OF THE MAGICAL...

MAURICE CHEVALIER

le sous-marin vert
(YELLOW SUBMARINE)

broadway
oui, au whisky
sourire aux lèvres

Recorded but rejected: 'Shirley's Wild Accordion'.

HOW I WON THE WAR

On the release of Dick Lester's film shot in Spain a year earlier, John makes the cover of the first issue of the American counter-culture magazine *Rolling Stone*. The photo shows him dressed as the character he plays, Private Gripweed.

Birth of Jason Starkey!

In a nostalgic exercise of self-mockery, in the video of 'Hello, Goodbye', they appear in their Sgt Pepper's outfits before briefly putting on their old grey suits circa 1963 and adopting the poses of Dezo Hoffmann's photos...

THE BEATLES
Hello, Goodbye / I am the Walrus

Single/November 67/Parlophone.

Rarely has a single had two sides that contrast so much.
While Paul offers his idiotic, very "bubble gum" but quite addictive song, John on the B-side, gives us a blazing, desperate, surreal song, composed under the influence of LSD and magically arranged by George Martin.

Though they complement each other perfectly, it's quite schizophrenic, so totally at odds are the creative directions taken by John and Paul.

THE BEATLES
Magical mystery tour

2xEP/December 67/Parlophone

The film's original soundtrack had too many songs for an EP and not enough for a whole album. Never mind, it's released in Europe as a double deluxe EP with an illustrated booklet. The Beatles are denied nothing, especially after the success of Sgt Pepper's.

There is good and bad in these new songs. First those that disappoint: 'Flying', an instrumental composed by all four, is the worst thing the Beatles have ever done, and 'Blue Jay Way' by George Harrison is moronic, sluggish and repetitive.

The best song on the record is the final song, 'I Am The Walrus', John's only contribution to this project, but of very fine vintage.

Magical Mystery Tour was released as an album in the USA by adding all the unreleased singles that came out in 1967. That greatly improved the overall quality!

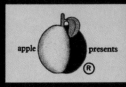

apple presents

This bizarre logo appears on the sleeve. But what is it?

December 4: opening of the Apple boutique, 94 Baker Street, London W1.

This is the first stone of the business structure devised by the Beatles after Brian Epstein's death.

They sell everything in here, clothes, ornaments and hippie accessories. The entire London pop scene is there. There are masses of people. A BBC commentator faints because of the heat and lack of air.

The psychedelic mural on the outside is not appreciated in this bourgeois area. The residents protest.

THE FOOL

The concert promoter Sid Bernstein's offer of $1 million for the Beatles to go back on stage is categorically refused by those concerned.

FLOP?

THE BBC BROADCASTS *MAGICAL MYSTERY TOUR* AT CHRISTMAS, IN BLACK AND WHITE, THUS SABOTAGING ITS PSYCHEDELIC ELEMENT. THE CRITICS LASH OUT.

JOHN HOLDS PAUL RESPONSIBLE FOR THIS FIRST MAJOR FAILURE IN THE BAND'S CAREER.

CHRISTMAS TIME IS HERE AGAIN

The sleeve of the new Rolling Stones album, released at the end of the year, is slightly embarrassing... the record also, at times. 1967 was not the year of the Stones.

JAI GURU DEVA OM

February: before their departure for India, EMI asks them to record at least one single. This is done. John's 'Across The Universe' is also recorded. To sing the chorus, two fans (Lizzy Bravo and Gayleen Pearse) are chosen from among the dozens who permanently hang around outside the studio.

Ashram

Amidst light-fingered monkeys, our friends, accustomed to a luxurious lifestyle in recent years, meditate in bungalows with no electricity. John is disappointed that yogi flight is not taught here.

The German band Tangerine Dream is born, its name taken from 'Lucy In The Sky...'

George is on top form as 1968 gets under way.

After the fame and the millions, the Beatles follow their mystic Benjamin in search of serenity beside the Maharishi.

RISHIKESH

Mid-February, the Beatles leave by plane for a meditation workshop that will last a few weeks or perhaps forever, if they like it. The journey seems never ending, but they finally arrive completely exhausted at the foot of the Himalayas. The place is amazing.

Dear Prudence

Among the other "students" at Rishikesh are the actress Mia Farrow and her sister Prudence, who worries everybody by meditating all day long, locked in her room.

Ah Ommm

APART FROM MEDITATING AND ATTENDING THE MAHARISHI'S LECTURES, THERE IS NOT MUCH TO DO AT RISHIKESH.

JOHN AND PAUL COMPOSE DOZENS OF SONGS.

Among the other seminarians are the very reactionary Mike Love from the Beach Boys and Donovan, the "British Dylan", who teaches claw-hammer finger-picking guitar techniques to John and Paul.

Yer Blues

Haunted by Yoko Ono who writes him passionate letters almost daily, John begins to suffer from insomnia and sinks into depression. He confesses his infidelity to Cynthia.

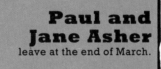

THE BEATLES
Lady Madonna / The inner light

Single/March 68/Parlophone

Back to the source of rock for this 'Lady Madonna', pure Paul, slightly parodic, marking the end of the band's psychedelic period.
George, for the first time, is the writer of the B-side, with this pretty raga perfectly in tune with what the Beatles are now into.

Lennon arrived too late with 'Hey Bulldog', which would have given this single even more balls.

Ringo and Maureen

are the first to leave after 13 days. They miss their kids and western food too much.

"I said it was like Butlin's holiday camp," says Ringo when he arrives in London.

Paul and Jane Asher

leave at the end of March.

John, George

and their wives

leave the ashram on April 12, furious, having been told by their new guru, Magic Alex, that the Maharishi was chatting up Mia Farrow.

Frank Zappa's Mothers Of Invention are the first to pastiche the sleeve of *Sgt Pepper's* for their new album *We're Only In It For The Money.*

Magic Alex!

The Greek Alexis Mardas is the Beatles' new guru. John is fascinated by him, and entrusts him with the Electronics department at Apple. John met the ex-TV engineer in the Indica gallery, where he was exhibiting his kinetic works. Alex begins work on the Apple recording studio, which should be revolutionary. A 72-track tape machine! An invisible field of sonic force! And a flying saucer! (true)

The record label Apple is launched in great style! Neil Aspinall, the ex-roadie from 1963, is made director.

WHAT'S THE NEW MARY JANE?

What's the new Mary Jane? Buried, the apathetic John of 1967. The conquering Lennon is back, determined not to compromise his integrity.

May 20:

YOKO ONO
小野 洋子

John and Yoko record experimental music then spend the night together. From the next day on, "Johnandyoko" become a pair of lovebirds.

End of May:
Album session 1968
The Beatles wrote enough material in India to fill a double album! But from the start the ambience is tense. John needs the continual presence of Yoko, his new muse, in the studio. He and Yoko work on 'Revolution No 9', an experimental piece more than eight minutes long. "The new direction of the band," John asserts to an aggrieved Paul.

BER 9 ··· NUMBER 9 ··· NUMBER 9 ··· NUMBER 9 ··· NUMBER 9 ··· NUMBER 9

George and Jane Birkin are in Cannes presenting the film *Wonderwall*. Ringo accompanies his mate.

HELTER SKELTER
(July)

While Paul irritates all his band mates for a month with his annoying Caribbean tune 'Ob-la-di Ob-la-da', he comes up with the Beatles heaviest titles ever. The bass player has read in NME that 'I Can See For Miles' by The Who is the most raucous song ever recorded. Jealous without even having heard it, Paul decides to go one better. Or worse.

May 18: John invites everybody to Apple to announce he is really Jesus Christ.

PUSHING THE BUTTONS

July 16: the tense atmosphere of the sessions and the disagreeable attitude of the Beatles towards him make Geoff Emerick, the band's sound engineer, crack up. He leaves the sinking ship. As for George Martin, he can stand it no longer. Besides, nobody's listening to him nowadays since the Beatles became the producers of their own records.

This man has talent...

One day he sang his songs to a tape recorder (borrowed from the man next door). In his neatest handwriting he wrote an explanatory note (giving his name and address) and, remembering to enclose a picture of himself, sent the tape, letter and photograph to *apple* music, 94 Baker Street, London, W.1. If you were thinking of doing the same thing yourself - do it now!
This man now owns a Bentley!

Robert Fraser, Paul's friend who runs an art gallery, sells him a Magritte painting, "Le jeu de Mourre" (The game of Mora). Apple's definitive logo has been found.

July 31: repainted white for a while now the Apple boutique, a financial drain, closes its doors. The stock is distributed to passers-by:
one item per person, please.

CAVENDISH AVENUE
(Paul's house)

Victoria Park

Regent's park

ABBEY ROAD
EMI studios

BBC

APPLE BOUTIQUE, Baker St

EMI

APPLE, Wigmore St

BAG O'NAILS

AD LIB

INDICA

Hyde Park

Thames

London

Heathrow airport

London

Richmond

Bushy

Wimbledon

KENWOOD
(John's house)

WEYBRIDGE

KINFAUNS
(George)

SUNNY EIGHTS
(Ringo)

ESHER

July 17:
premiere of
the animated film
YELLOW SUBMARINE.

The Beatles
record
'YER BLUES'
in the broom
cupboard of
Abbey Road
Studio 1!

LOVE

August 30: The Fabs spend the day being photographed by Robert Whittaker.

bye, Ringo

On August 22, Ringo leaves the band for two reasons, according to him: "I'm not playing well and I feel unloved."

Paul immediately replaces him on the drums, notably on 'Back In The USSR'.

The sessions have been going on for three months now. Each records his own songs and the others are used simply as session musicians…

Paul likes kids.

He likes to play with them, which impresses John. Paul often comes to see Julian, now four years old, after his parents have separated. He has written a song for him, and it will be the next Beatles single.

Hey Jude!

To test its impact, Paul has painted the name of the next single on a window of the Apple boutique. There is disquiet among the neighbours who think it is an anti-Semitic slogan!

You like The Beatles? You might also like:

ODESSEY and ORACLE

THE ZOMBIES

September 6:

ERIC CLAPTON

plays the solo on 'While My Guitar Gently Weeps', on which his friend George Harrison had slaved for eight hours, in vain, the night before.

He will be credited "Eddie Clayton" for contractual reasons.

🐞🐞🐞🐞🐞 + 🐞!

THE BEATLES
Hey Jude / Revolution

Single/August 68/Apple

- -

'Hey Jude' was composed for Julian. A seven-minute song that created problems for the technicians who had to compress the first part in order to make it fit onto one side of a single. Some scoff that the title is symptomatic of the Beatles' silly side, Paul fashion.

It is difficult, however, not to be carried away by the second part, quite epic. The song progresses, gets more intense and, to be honest, without any sense of shame, after a few minutes, one feels an irrepressible urge to sing "nanana" at the top of one's voice.

Or you don't have a heart.

The B-side is the antithesis of the A-side. Sound-effects rock, engaged, even if one doesn't always get John's message ("When you talk about destruction, don't you know that you can count me out", really?) A number one in 11 countries as soon as it is released, even in France!

'Hey Jude' is among the first batch of Apple records, along with 'Those Were The Days' by Mary Hopkin, 'Thingumybob' by the Black Dyke Mills band, produced by Paul, and 'Sour Milk Sea' by Jackie Lomax, produced by George.

John and Yoko convicted of possession of cannabis.

In the first biography of the band, we learn that Pete Best is working in the biscuit section of Woolworths

STARR IS BACK

Cynthia obtains her divorce.

Ringo returns 15 days after his departure. Feeling sheepish, the other three have filled Studio 1 with flowers to welcome him.

This time it was by the skin of their teeth.

Wonderwall Music By George Harrison — Apple Records

♪♪♪♪♪

GEORGE HARRISON
Wonderwall music

LP/November 68/Apple

An original soundtrack of a little known but absolutely superb film.

Between Indian music recorded in Bombay at the beginning of the year, George has composed attractive instrumentals, often moving, at times very rock ('Microbes') which testify, if still necessary, to the expanding talent of the youngest member of the band.

♪♪♪♪♪ + ♪!

JOHN LENNON & YOKO ONO
Unfinished Music No1: Two Virgins

LP/November 68/Apple

The music on offer here is either interesting and audacious - or ultra complacent and tedious. In the name of love!

Next to it, 'Revolution Number 9' sounds like Chuck Berry.

Full marks for the absolutely mythic sleeve, concealed in the USA by a discreet brown envelope and released on the small label Tetragrammaton.

Linda Eastman,

a 27-year-old New York photographer settles in London.

For the last few months she's been having a relationship with Paul McCartney, who not so long ago was talking about getting engaged to Jane Asher…

'Z' is for Zapple.

Introducing Zapple, a new label from Apple Records.

Zapple is the sub-label of Apple, dedicated to experimental projects.

Directed by Barry Miles, the soul of Indica, it will welcome the crazier projects promoted by the Beatles and their friends, and also recordings by writers (Brautigan and Bukowski already planned) as well as political speeches (Mao, Castro…).

DIRTY MAC

is the name of the supergroup made up of John Lennon, Keith Richards, Eric Clapton and Mitch Mitchell, which plays 'Yer Blues' during the Rock'n'roll Circus, a TV show conceived by the Rolling Stones, which was shelved because the Stones played badly.

♫♫♫♫♫ + ♫ !

THE BEATLES
The Beatles

2 x LP/November 68/Apple

- -

A white 30cm square object. The Beatles appears in embossed letters on the front.

Each is numbered. John Lennon has managed to get number 000001.
Inside, two records with a green apple in the centre, cut open on the reverse side. There is a poster, a collage of photos signed by Richard Hamilton, who also designed the sleeve. The Pepper years are definitely over.

On the poster, among other stuff, Ringo can be seen dancing with Liz Taylor. Classy. There are also four portraits on art paper. They are now four hairy boys. One of them is wearing round glasses.

At the beginning of the record a plane takes off, to introduce 30 songs in which the range of styles is vast, from Caribbean music to heavy rock, from an improvised ballad to an ultra-orchestrated song. It's incredible to think that such a rich work could result from such uptight and chaotic sessions.

This is the Beatles White Album. It is the most popular double album of its time, the only masterpiece on which a quarter of the songs are quite unnecessary, including one that is unlistenable, but we cherish regardless!

Other sleeve ideas, including the Beatles carved on Mt Rushmore, were abandoned.

Phew!

Martha is Paul's two-year-old Old English sheepdog

Martha!

Yoko is hospitalised for a miscarriage. John stays with her day and night (he sleeps on the floor).

Three London concerts planned for Beatles stage comeback – stop – but failure of Paul to persuade the others back on stage – stop –

Christmas!

From California, Hells Angels burst into Apple, in London. They settle into the offices and terrorise the staff. George has to use all his hippie diplomatic skills to make them leave.

It was he who had invited them!

Christmas 1968 record with Tiny Tim as guest!

CHRISTMAS 1968

FROM THE PHOTOS OF
RICHARD AVEDON.

69

January 2: first day of the shoot in Twickenham. The Beatles rehearsals are filmed day in day out by Michael Lindsay-Hogg for a new documentary.

They prepare for a concert that will take place in Tripoli's ancient circus, and become the climax of the film.

They will perform only new songs.

A bearded McCartney tries to instil some enthusiasm, but his monologues verge on the ridiculous while the other three seem to be sleeping.

He is directing the sessions but his authoritarian attitude begins to grate on everyone's nerves...

The project turns sour very quickly. They have to start playing at 8a.m. in a poorly heated hanger, and having just finished the White Album they seem exhausted.

Yoko is never further than 2cm from John, who appears not to care. The couple are going through their

SEX, CAVIAR & HEROIN
period.

The Biteulz? They add Charleston pedals to Faure's harmonies.

> **"I'll play whatever you want me to play, or I won't play at all if you don't want me to play."**

10 January 10:
George Harrison leaves the band after the umpteenth altercation with McCartney. A delighted Yoko hopes to take his place!

In the end George comes back on the 15th, laying down his conditions:

-- The concert plans are abandoned.
-- An album with new songs will be made.
-- Freezing Twickenham is abandoned.

• **January 20:**
they move into the Apple studios which Magic Alex is supposed to have completed. Unfortunately, Alex has done nothing and it is unusable. George Martin and the EMI mobile studio are called to the rescue.

Magic Alex's installation is later sold to an electronics scrap dealer for a fiver.

3 Savile Row, London W.1.

THE BEATLES
Yellow Submarine

LP/January 69/Apple

Six months after the cinema release of this superb psychedelic animated film, its soundtrack is finally released too. Showing little interest in the project for fear it will be little more than a long version of the 1965 mediocre cartoons, our friends offer only four original songs recorded between 1967 and 68. 'Hey Bulldog' is great. George Martin's orchestral music fills the B-side.

A missed chance, an oddity in the Beatles discography.

> "Apple is losing money. If it carries on like this, we'll be broke in six months."

John in Disc & *Music Echo*.

GET BACK!

They start recording again from scratch. It is a brilliant idea to invite organ player Billy Preston to flesh out the sound. In his presence, the Beatles stop arguing and play their best.

Finally,

there is a concert to end the 'Get Back' sessions.

On January 30, on the roof of number 3, Savile Row, The Beatles plug in their guitars and play in the freezing cold in front of the Apple staff and folk from neighbouring offices. After 42 minutes the police intervene and unplug the sound system... much to Ringo's dismay, as he would like to have been taken away in a Black Maria. It would have made a great finale for the film!

Sgt pepper's

finally drops out of the Billboard charts in March 1969 after 88 weeks.

A few titles recorded during the Get Back sessions:

Some covers:
Besame Mucho (!) • Blue Suede Shoes • Bye Bye Love • Going Up The Country • Lawdy Miss Clawdy • Love Me Do (!) • Milkman Bring Me No More Blues • Miss Ann • Not Fade Away • Save The Last Dance For Me • Shake, Rattle & Roll • Tracks Of My Tears.

Some new songs: *All Things Must Pass • Bathroom Window • Billy's Song (Billy Preston) • I Want You • Isn't It A Pity • Just A Child Of Nature • Rocker • Oh Darling • Teddy Boy*

Allen Klein

John and Yoko fall under the spell of the Stones' American ex-manager who is regarded as very astute. He becomes the Beatles' manager for 20% of their income.

Mick Jagger warns Paul to beware of the guy.

Paul refuses to sign and entrusts his father-in-law, Lee Eastman, with looking after his business affairs.

That doesn't help the relationship between our four friends, knives are drawn.

Wedding 1.

On March 12, Paul marries Linda Eastman. The fans, in tears, try to molest the bride.

Wedding 2.

By a strange coincidence, John and Yoko get married on March 20 in Gibraltar.

A few days later, John officially becomes JOHN ONO WINSTON LENNON.

THE BEATLES with BILLY PRESTON
Get back / Don't let me down

Single/April 69/Apple

An A-side rock number by Paul, and a more bluesy B-side by John, now visibly stressed. And paranoiac too, for he thought that 'Get Back' was addressed to Yoko, whom Paul was looking at while singing the chorus.

Two excellent titles through and through, quite representative of the 'Live without fiddling' sound of the 'Get Back' sessions.

Number one just about everywhere.

Give Peace A Chance.

The famous couple choose to hold their honeymoon in public, in hotels in Amsterdam and Montreal where, for days on end, from 9 in the morning to 9 in the evening they welcome the media and many friends to talk about peace in the world.

Hoping they were going to make love in front of the cameras, some journalists leave, disappointed.

JOHN LENNON & YOKO ONO
Unfinished music N°2 : Life with the lions

LP/May 69/Zapple

GEORGE HARRISON
Electronic sound

LP/May 69/Zapple

Simultaneous release of the two first (and last) records of the sub-label Zapple.

At times the first offers a kind of shrill and tired free jazz. The second allows us to hear George's first attempts at composing on his Moog synthesizer that has just been delivered. He seems to have a jolly good time, us less so.

Back To Business

Concerned about tensions within the band and John's erratic behaviour, Dick James, the Beatles music publisher, sells his share of Northern Songs to ATV, which now holds the majority.

A battle for ownership follows, which The Beatles lose.

The Beatles no longer own their songs.

Taken in hand

Allen Klein spring cleans Apple. He fires staff left right and centre and studies the accounts.

Apple had a very rock'n'roll way of functioning... The cost of 'illegal' cigarettes and alcohol was monumental.

The employees' favourite sport was pillaging. Gold records, typewriters, furniture... A family of Californian hippies camped in reception.

Finally Zapple is closed down and Magic Alex fired. He has cost the company almost £300,000 without any of his "inventions" actually working.

"He was given the shittiest load of badly recorded shit with a lousy feeling to it ever, and he made something out of it." – John Lennon

On May 28, the album Get Back is ready. For the sleeve, the Beatles pose in the stairwell of EMI, as they had in 1963 for their first LP. It isn't used. The Beatles reject a mix by Glyn Johns, who replaced George Martin. The sound is judged too poor, and there is a risk the public won't like it. The record is put on stand-by...

July 1969

To his great surprise, George Martin is asked by the Beatles to produce a new album "old-fashioned style", in the EMI studios. Paul assures him that everybody is motivated, "even John" (which is not true). The boys don't want to bow out with the failure of the 'Get Back' sessions.

BED

It starts badly. John and Yoko miss the first nine days of recording because of a car accident. Paul, George and Ringo think they are hallucinating when a bed is delivered to the studio for Yoko, still convalescing. Bad vibrations are back.

THE BEATLES
The ballad of John and Yoko / Old brown shoe

Single/May 68/Apple

Considering their declining relationship, John and Paul put their differences aside to record this song about John & Yoko which was written and recorded in one day by them alone, the other two being absent. The verse "They're gonna crucify me" results in a ban on American radio.

The B-side, by George, is worthwhile, especially its hysterical 'Hey Bulldog'-style finale.

GEORGE HAS HIS MOOG DELIVERED TO THE STUDIOS. IT CAN BE HEARD ON SEVERAL SONGS,, NOTABLY 'I WANT YOU' (THE FAMOUS WHITE NOISE AT THE END).

In the end, even though the quarrels are scarcer, combined work is also rare. Each works on his own songs. John is against the idea of the side two medley but will go with the flow.

GIVE PEACE A CHANCE / Remember love

PLASTIC ONO BAND ♡Apple

PLASTIC ONO BAND
Give peace a chance / Remember love

Single/July 69/Apple

This long mantra is THE peace hymn par excellence, recorded on June 1, 1969 during the bed-in in Montreal. The chorus is chanted by those present in the hotel room, among them the LSD guru Timothy Leary, Allen Ginsberg, a few Krishna devotees, and plenty of others, including a CIA agent dressed as a hippie.

It is the first record by John & Yoko's infinitely variable new group, the Plastic Ono Band.

THE END

To finish the medley, Paul convinces Ringo, who's in a panic, to perform a kind of drum solo, the first in his Beatles career. Then Paul, John & George put aside their quarrels to record, in one take, a "duel" of solo guitars.

It's the last time they play together.

"EVEREST"

That's the title this album should have had, after Geoff Emerick's brand of cigarettes. For the sleeve, Paul had imagined a photo of the band taken at the top of the famous mountain. But it's not the time for such excesses.

On the morning of August 8, our four hairy friends cross the road near the Abbey Road studios for photographer Iain McMillan.

It has to be done fast, as the police only halt the traffic for a few minutes.

August 9: Charles Manson receives a "call to murder" while listening to the White Album. He has Roman Polanski's wife, Sharon Tate, then pregnant, murdered by his disciples. On the walls PIGS and HELTER SKELTER are written with the victims' blood.

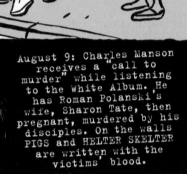

On August 22, looking serious, the Beatles pose for their last ever photo session at Tittenhurst Park, the huge Georgian house near Ascot that John and Yoko have bought.

At Woodstock, Joe Cocker becomes famous with his epileptic cover of 'With A Little Help From My Friends'.

♪♪♪♪♪

THE BEATLES
Abbey road

LP/September 69/Apple

- -

Am I dreaming or hasn't he given top marks to Abbey Road? Who does he think he is, that idiot?

Okay, side one is the art of extremes, the ravine between 'Octopus's Garden' and 'I Want You' is slightly annoying. But the second side, Good God, the medley! It's magical! And the dramatic finale! And 'Her Majesty', the first hidden track in history, used for its downplayed end? Harrison, having reached maturity and full of confidence, has the two best songs on the album. And what about the mythical sleeve?

Well, 'Maxwell's Silver Hammer' is truly unbearable. And 'Oh! Darling' is a tad forced as a pastiche, but holy mackerel Batman, it's Abbey Road!
Let us not touch the Beatles best album. Bastard.

Signed: a stricken reader.

- -

BANG ! BANG !

On 'Maxwell's Silver Hammer'
Paul evokes the 'pataphysics'
of French writer Alfred Jarry,
creator of Ubu Roi.

Is Paul dead?

is the rumour spread by the American DJ Russ Gibb. Paul would have died at the wheel of his Aston Martin in August 1966. Hence the end of touring and the arrival of the moustaches to hide the scars of plastic surgery, for he has been replaced by a look-alike.

One can find clues in some songs:
-- "Paul is dead, miss him, miss him" says John at the end of 'I'm So Tired'.
-- "Turn me on, dead man" can be heard if one reverses a passage in 'Revolution No 9'.
-- "He blew his mind out in a car" in 'A Day In The Life'.

And on the sleeves:
-- The hand of Death on Paul's head on Sgt Pepper.
-- He wears an armband "OPD" (officially pronounced dead).
-- On Abbey Road, he has a cigarette in his right hand, while he is left-handed.
-- On the plate of the Volkswagon Beetle: LMW28. "Living McCartney would be 28".
Well, you know, he was 27 in 1969.

September 5: meeting at Apple.

Allen Klein has re-negotiated the contract with EMI. Good news. Paul starts to talk about the future but to each proposition he makes, John says "no". He announces he is leaving the band and will keep quiet about it as long as the business requires it.

John leaves the band.

Plastic Ono Band
COLD TURKEY
Don't worry Kyoko
(Mummy's only looking for a hand in the snow)

HYPERACTIVE

-- In October, John goes back on stage at the Toronto Rock Festival.
-- In November, he sends back his MBE medal to protest against British politics in Biafra and... against 'Cold Turkey' slipping down the charts.
-- The release of the Plastic Ono Band's single 'What's The New Mary Jane'/'You Know My Name' is blocked by the other three. It was actually a Beatles recording.

PLASTIC ONO BAND
Cold Turkey / Don't worry Kyoko

Single/October 69/Apple

- -

'Cold Turkey' is a funky rock number, harsh and piercing, rejected by Paul as the next Beatles single. Lennon screams about his addiction to heroin, and it ends with cries of orgasm (or pain) amid feedback.
Good radical Lennon.
Slightly gruelling.

It seems as if a goat is being slaughtered on the B-side. Oh dear, silly me, it's Yoko hooting!

KINKS

You like the Beatles, you will also like Arthur by the Kinks.

In November, the magazine LIFE reassures its fans.

Paul McCartney is alive and well.

He has been living for weeks as a recluse with his family on his Scottish farm.

In reality, John's decision to leave the Beatles has shattered him. He has remained in bed for days, incapable of getting up, on the edge of despair.

A Beatle for nearly 10 years, he can't accept the still unofficial separation.

LIFE

THE CASE OF THE 'MISSING' BEATLE
Paul is still with us

A LOST ALBUM

The September 17 issue of Rolling Stone reports on rumours of a Beatles album recorded between February and May 1969 and called Hot As Sun. The tapes apparently had been stolen from the EMI studio. The band decided to forget it and record another that became Abbey Road.

Beat
BOOK

WITH INFORMATION BECOMING SCARCE, THE LAST ISSUE OF THE BEATLES BOOK MONTHLY APPEARS IN DECEMBER '69.

McCartney

Around Christmas,
in utmost secrecy,
Paul starts recording his first
solo album in the attic of his
Cavendish Avenue house, using a
four-track recorder on loan
and without a mixing desk.

He plays all
the instruments.

Happy Christmas From John & Yoko

At Christmas, in 11 big cities, John and Yoko finance the distribution of leaflets and the erection of huge posters promoting peace in the world.

PLASTIC ONO BAND
Live Peace in Toronto 1969

LP/December 69/Apple

- -

On September 13, John Lennon, suffering from stage fright, plays on stage at a Toronto festival, accompanied by Yoko, Eric Clapton, Klaus Voorman and Alan White. This is the result, on which John interprets his old rock'n'roll favourites as well as a few recent songs, while Yoko screams throughout her contributions.

A rehearsal and efficient tuning up wouldn't have gone amiss.

1970

YEAR ONE

At the beginning of January, John & Ono cut their hair and sell it to raise funds to help the activist Michael X.

I, Me, Mine.

On January 3 and 4, in John's absence, George, Paul and Ringo re-work George's song for inclusion on a new version of the 'Get Back' album, now re-named Let It Be, and finally scheduled for release.

LENNON
INSTANT KARMA!

APPLES 1003

TOP OF THE POPS!

A younger-looking and overexcited John plays 'Instant Karma!' on the famous BBC programme.

Yoko, blindfolded, knits at his side...

♪♪♪♪♪+♪!

JOHN LENNON
Instant Karma! / Who has seen the wind?

Single/February 70/Apple

- -

Recorded at the end of January and released a week later. Lennon is at his best when a sense of urgency drives his work. A top-form Lennon in a state of grace, produced 1957-style by Phil Spector, his new sound guru.

On the centre of the disc, "PLAY LOUD" is written on the A-side, and "PLAY SOFT" on the B-side.

PHIL SPECTOR,

THE FAMOUS SIXTIES PRODUCER, HAS BEEN LOOKING TO MAKE HIS COMEBACK. IT'S A GODSEND FOR HIM WHEN LENNON AND KLEIN INVITE HIM TO REMIX THE LET IT BE ALBUM THAT HAS BEEN ON HOLD SINCE SPRING 1969.

On the left, Ringo and Maureen return from the US premier of the film *The Magic Christian*.

Six weeks before the planned release of *Let It Be*, Phil Spector remixes the album at Abbey Road.

SPECTOR

gets rid of the old rock covers and re-arranges many of the songs with strings. He adds dialogues from the film, female backing singers and even changes a few chords on 'The Long And Winding Road'. He seems possessed and shouts for more echo, more reverb. Ringo takes him aside and orders him to calm down.

Paul is appalled when he hears the new mix.

At the same time, in another studio reserved for a certain "Billy Martin", McCartney discreetly puts the final touches to his solo album.

• 1st April •
It is announced that John and Yoko have changed sex.

Ringo rings Paul's doorbell to ask him to postpone the release of his album. Paul throws him out.

BREAK?

In a letter that accompanies the promo copies of his album, Paul answers a questionnaire. The answers are laconic and cynical

-- Is your break with the Beatles temporary?
-- I don't know. There are personal and musical conflicts.
-- Are you preparing a new album with the Beatles?
-- No.

Hunter Davies confirms that the group has split up "because of Yoko".

Apple denies the fact in The Times. But nobody believes it any longer.

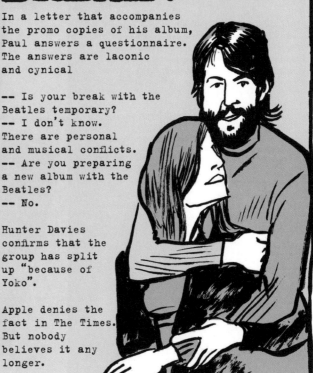

🐾🐾🐾🐾🐾
PAUL McCARTNEY
McCartney

LP/April 70/Apple

The first solo album by Paul is a bizarre work, especially after the very slick and craftsmanlike Abbey Road. John Lennon is flabbergasted that Paul, the perfectionist of the Beatles (and ultra-demanding with his companions!), releases a solo album with such lack of sophistication.

Only one song seems to have been produced in a manner worthy of Paul's old band, the extraordinary and dramatic 'Maybe I'm Amazed'. The rest seem more like demos for a forthcoming Beatles album, which is not such a bad thing after all!

Recorded and produced alone (with "lovely" Linda doing backing vocals here and there), McCartney is a unique record whose gloomy and minimalist atmosphere holds us spellbound and puzzles us a bit more at each listening.

The bizarre sound in the intro of 'Glasses' is a wet finger dragged across a wine glass.

And the baby in the jacket is Paul and Linda's daughter Mary, eight months old.

"I STARTED THE BAND. I DISBANDED IT. IT'S AS SIMPLE AS THAT!"

John, who had left the band months ago but was keeping quiet about it, is furious that Paul announces the end of the Beatles.

1. Charles Hawtrey
(actor)
2. Matt Busby
(footballer and manager)
3. Doris Day
(actress)

🐾🐾🐾🐾🐾
THE BEATLES
Let it be

LP/May 70/Apple

The therapeutic treatment.

Started in January 1969 in Twickenham, continued in Savile Row.

Mixed by Glyn Johns. Rejected. Spectorized one year later to try to save a project moribund since its birth, the ill-advised plan to film the creation of a new Beatles album. Finally, after those equivocations, what's left of that album recorded before Abbey Road but released six months later?

A few good songs ('Two Of Us'). Others not so good ('For You Blue'). Others still not completed, not to say not really started ('Dig It'). Some violins, to hide the misery. Not much juice. Spoken interludes. Hits ('Let It Be', released as a single before Phil's remix, with the famous 'You Know My Name' from 1967 as B-side).

A wasted opportunity.

A slightly mouldy way to finish a story which, until now, is immaculate.

P.S. this record was originally available in a box that also contained a nice (fragile) book of photos of the film.

LET IT BE

an intimate bioscopic experience with
THE BEATLES

The film is released on the May 20. No Beatle is at the premiere. That's understandable, so many bad memories.

However, it is fascinating to see for ourselves the biggest band in the world working, creating as best they could and moving ineluctably towards the split.

A beautiful sad film.

APPLE
An abkco managed company
presents

"Let it be"

Produced by NEIL ASPINAL Directed by MICHAEL LINDSAY-HOGG

MOTION PICTURE SCORE
LE ON APPLE RECORDS

While their contract is supposed to run until 1976, Paul requests in writing the official dissolution of the band.

PRIMAL Scream

John, passionate about Dr Arthur Janov's book, starts a course of therapy with the psychologist in order to cure himself of his neurosis and addictions. He spends his days screaming and crying to get rid of the tension he has accumulated since his childhood. The primal therapy is supposed to last 15 months but after four and a big argument, the therapist loses his best client.

John Lennon records the excellent 'Do The Oz' to help the underground magazine Oz which is in difficulties.

In his "Rubrique-à-Brac" in the magazine Pilote, Marcel Gotlib gives his opinion on the split....

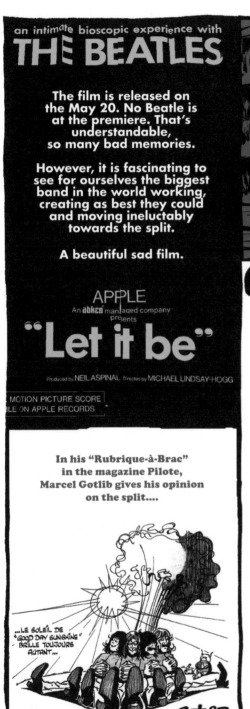

...LE SOLEIL DE "GOOD DAY SUNSHINE" BRILLE TOUJOURS AUTANT...

Gotlib

RINGO STARR
Sentimental journey

LP/March 70/Apple

- -

RINGO STARR
Beaucoups of blues

LP/September 70/Apple

- -

We couldn't wait for Ringo's first two solo albums, and here they are. The first, "made for his mum", is a compilation of old tunes arranged by various producers, among them George Martin. Beautiful sleeve.

The second, much more interesting, features covers of country songs, a genre much liked by the drummer, and it's not at all bad.

A very talented clone of Paul McCartney.

EMITT RHODES

JOHN LENNON
Plastic Ono band

LP/December 70/Apple

- -

YOKO ONO
Plastic Ono band

LP/December 70/Apple

- -

Recorded after his primal therapy, this first solo album by John without Yoko is directly influenced by the traumatic and cathartic experience. It is co-produced by Phil Spector, but apart from a bit of an echo here and there, it is difficult to imagine anything more dry and sober. Guitar-bass-drums-piano-voice. Full stop.

Lennon screams or whispers about the death of his mother, cries about being abandoned by his father, and confides in us that he no longer believes in God or the Beatles.
He is an artist at his most sincerely raw, and it is deeply moving.

Unusually, Yoko's record has the same sleeve and the same title as that of her husband. Though it doesn't match the quality of John's LP, it remains the first audible piece by the Japanese artist.

GEORGE

has been told his mother, Louise, has died during the long but agreeable recording of his first solo album in Trident studios. Most of these new songs had been turned down by Paul or John in 1968-1969…

GEORGE HARRISON
ALL THINGS MUST PASS

The "garden gnomes" sleeve photo was taken in the grounds of George's extravagant new home, Friar Park at Henley-on-Thames. The mansion used to belong to the eccentric Sir Frankie Crisp, a horticulture fanatic, who became the subject of one of George's later songs.

GEORGE HARRISON
All things must pass

3 x LP/November 70/Apple

Unlike his hierarchical ex-superiors Paul and John, George Harrison has decided to launch his solo career in an upfront manner, without humility. Humility was starting to piss him off!

This mammoth album is the fruit of 10 years of frustration and humiliation and George means to show the world what he is capable of. Hence a triple album, brimming with hits, in an impressive box. The sound offered by Spector is fat and full, heavy enough for a Krishna to choke on it.

Also impressive is the profusion and quality of his compositions, from the epic 'What Is Life' to the delicate 'Isn't It A Pity', down to the proto-disco 'Art Of Dying'.

Take note though that the third record, composed of long jam sessions, is as relevant as any record of jam sessions… it's a bit tedious. .

Taking everybody by surprise, this "triple black" sold many more copies than the records by the other ex-Beatles.

The revenge of the youngest!

George responds to the rumours of reforming. "Who knows? Stranger things can happen."

PAUL sends a handwritten letter to the Melody Maker to put a stop to the rumours of the Beatles reforming.

fig 1. *Scarabaeoidea (Scarab)*

THE BEATLES - 1960 1970

71

GEORGE

barely has time to savour his international success before he is charged with plagiarism. 'My Sweet Lord' bears too much resemblance to the Chiffons' 'He's So Fine' (1963).

18/02/71:

Paul, who for the occasion has put on his old Abbey Road suit again, is forced to summon the other three Beatles to appear in court. He demands the legal dissolution of the band and an audit of their accounts.

War against Allen Klein and his ex-bandmates is declared.

Strangely enough it is Paul & Linda who receive the Grammy Award for Let It Be, presented by a drunken John Wayne.

Bashful lover?

Inspired by his unrequited love for Pattie, George's wife, Eric Clapton writes the beautiful 'Layla'.

"The Beatles are the biggest bastards on earth"

Interviewed at length by Rolling Stone editor Jann Wenner, John talks candidly about the end of the Beatles, LSD, primal scream, Yoko… and takes the opportunity to poke fun at Paul, George Martin, the Abbey Road medley and even George Harrison's album.

Ringo Starr
It Don't Come Easy/Early 1970

Single/April 71/Apple

Of course it's slightly laboured and everything is said after 50 seconds, but, to be honest, Ringo's first single, recorded more than a year before, is decent enough. Well, it was co-written and produced by George Harrison, with Stephen Stills and Klaus Voorman as well as Badfinger participating in the recording.

Unfortunately, in the video promo, it's obvious that Ringo hasn't made any progress in his ski-ing since *Help!*

PAUL McCARTNEY
Another day / Oh woman oh why

Single/February 71/Apple

The first single from Paul McCartney with Linda as backing singer.

Pure Macca, elegant, light and spring-like.

And a B-side that invents AC/DC.

A record adopted by the public, but slated by the critics who think that Led Zeppelin or Deep Purple are the best bands in the world.

JOHN LENNON / PLASTIC ONO BAND
Power to the people / Open your box

Single/March 71/Apple

Another dazzling single, quasi composed and recorded the day of its release! However, unlike 'Instant Karma', it doesn't really work.

The lefty-popular-seeking slogan-chorus in the mould of Give Peace A Chance adds to Spector's slightly clumsy sound and Yoko's B-side is preferable though quite trying. Lennon quickly judged this single "embarrassing".

YOKO ONO
Fly

2 x LP/March 71/Apple

Alas! A double album by Yoko! Have pity on us!

You'd better think again! Contrary to the previous recordings by the Lady, this record is exciting. Difficult, irritating, yes, but fascinating. A lot less complacent and boring than Unfinished Music, for example. Fly invents a whole section of New York underground rock five years before everybody else. I'm telling you. There are even real songs on it!

• COLLIDING CIRCLES •
• LEFT IS RIGHT •
• PINK LITMUS PAPER SHIRT •
• DECK CHAIR •

FOUR UNRELEASED BEATLES SONGS FROM THE REVOLVER PERIOD THAT DEDICATED FANS SEEK OUT ON PIRATE RECORDINGS, THUS BUILDING UP COUNTLESS MYTHS ABOUT THEM. YOUNG MUSIC JOURNALIST MARTIN LEWIS CONFESSES HE STARTED THE RUMOUR. THESE SONGS NEVER EXISTED!

🐏🐏🐏🐏🐏+🐏!

PAUL & LINDA McCARTNEY
Ram

LP/May 71/Apple
- -
On his Scottish farm near Campbelton, Kintyre, Paul McCartney, 29, raises animals and children. And he still writes as much as he ever did. But in spite of the success of his first album, he seems isolated. Voluntarily?

His image in the music milieu is that of a country bumpkin, and he likes to cultivate it. It is John who is the visionary, the revolutionary. Paul has sold out, he is dated.

Ram doesn't change anything. There are no crypto-maoist messages, no heavy-metal riffs. However, the album is exciting, with ukulele cameos, the "Buddy Holly-isms" and big songs in the style of Abbey Road with ad hoc production.

This silly sleeve hides a great album, less rustic and more ambitious than it appears. PS: Inside the gatefold, there is a photo of scarabs mating... A hidden message?

* Campbelton, Kintyre.

RAM
was recorded at the end of 1970 in New York with Denny Seiwell on drums, Linda adding backing vocals, and guitarists David Spinozza and Hugh McCraken.

Paul takes charge of the rest.

Paul and Linda have a farm of 100 acres, five horses, and 100 sheep that they shear themselves.

We don't know how many rams.

MOTHERS + PLASTIC ONO BAND
FILLMORE EAST, 5/6/71

🐏🐏🐏🐏🐏

GEORGE HARRISON
Bangla desh / Deep blue

Single/July 71/Apple
- -
Moved by conditions in Bangladesh, partly destroyed by a cyclone at the end of 1970, George, familiar with that corner of the planet, releases this single to raise money for the disaster fund. After a lachrymose start that doesn't bode well, the song takes flight after 20 seconds, and quickly makes you feel like dancing and crying at the same time.

The B-side is one of George's best songs, nothing less.

Concert for Bangladesh

The very first all-star charity rock concert takes place on August 1, organised by George Harrison at Madison Square Garden in New York. Over two shows 40,000 applaud George, as well as Ringo, Bob Dylan, Ravi Shankar, Eric Clapton, Leon Russell and many more. John Lennon refuses to come, having been told Yoko is not welcome... Paul is also invited but declines because Allen Klein is a co-organiser.

A whisker away from The Beatles reforming.

Apple Studios

Savile Row London W.1. 01-734 300

Wings !

Since 1966 Paul has been itching to tour again. To do so, he forms a new band, WINGS, with Linda and the two Dennys: Laine (ex-Moody Blues) and Seiwell, already on Ram. They rehearse in the Rude Studio, a shed at the bottom of the garden of his Scottish farm.

Imagine was recorded in June-July 1971 at John's home, Tittenhurst Park, and completed in New York. Several musicians took part, among them George Harrison, present on most of the titles.

JOHN LENNON
Imagine

LP/September 1971/Apple

From the point of view of its author, this album is a pop version of his previous LP. In so far as the previous one had absolutely nothing pop about it, in this respect they have nothing in common, other than that they are both excellent and produced by Spector, who this time brings in the heavy artillery, with a full orchestra and 1,000 pianos per song.

By turns pop and aggressive, John from the Beatles period is back. Political songs follow more sentimental material, like the utopian title-song much loved by the public. And proof that John has nothing to learn from Paul as far as soppiness is concerned!

The good songs are not lacking, like the hypnotic 'Gimme Some Truth' or 'Crippled Onside'. The album goes to number one in the USA.

This photo, a funny but cruel pastiche of Ram, was slipped into the sleeve of Imagine.

But in the song 'How Do You Sleep', his attack on Paul is more confrontational. This incredibly hateful song upset George and the other musicians present at the recording.

THIS IS NOT HERE

Exhibition by Yoko Ono in New York.

WINGS PARTY !

On November 8 at the very old-fashioned Empire Ballroom in London's Leicester Square Paul throws a party to launch his new band.

YOKO

has been fighting for three years for the custody of Kyoko, her daughter with her ex-husband, Anthony Cox.

After many ups and downs and an incredible kidnapping, Cox is sentenced to five days in jail for having refused to let Kyoko see her mother.

Cox and his daughter live in the community of the Church of the Living Word.

WINGS
Wild life

LP/December 71/Apple

Eight titles recorded in 15 days to launch Paul's group Wings and announce a tour for 1972.

Quite the opposite of the late period Beatles, these songs are supposed to be played live. Of course it's not Sgt Pepper's, it's not Ram either, it is a hybrid album, and that's part of its charm.

The last track, 'Dear Friend', alludes to John Lennon's attacks, without throwing oil on the fire. Paul knows full well that he would come out the loser in a squabble by song.

Beware, crappy sleeve, again.

Pink notebook

Stella McCartney is born on the 13/09/71. She is born by caesarean, and her dad prays to the angels that all will go well. It was while thinking about angels that he had an idea for a name for his band. Lennon must have had a good laugh when he was told the anecdote!

Ann Arbor, Michigan. John & Yoko take part in a concert to support John Sinclair, imprisoned for possessing two joints.

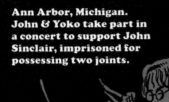

WAR IS (NOT) OVER

On December 4, John writes an acerbic open letter to Melody Maker. In it he responds to a recent interview by his ex-songwriting partner who said he found Imagine better than the previous album, because it was less political. John answers: "Imagine is 'Working Class Hero' with sugar on it for conservatives like yourself!!"

JOHN & YOKO
THE PLASTIC ONO BAND WITH THE HARLEM COMMUNITY CHOIR
Happy Xmas (War is over)

Single/December 71/Apple

A Spectorian Christmas song and a new episode in their crusade for peace, initiated by John & Ono in 1969.

It has all the qualities and the flaws of a Christmas song: nice to listen to at Christmas, surreal in the summer.

72 Que pasa New York?

Senator Strom Thurmond proposes the expulsion of John from the USA for possession of drugs. But it is more likely that his political activism is the real issue.

On February 5, 400 people protest against his expulsion. During the very popular Mike Douglas TV show, John and Yoko state that their phone is being tapped and that they are followed by the FBI.

The former star of Liverpudlian rock, Rory Storm, and his mother commit suicide together.

March mars : Fermeture
The Beatles fan club down.

🥾🥾🥾🤍🤍

Ringo Starr
It Don't Come Easy/Early 1970

3xLP/January 72/Apple

- -

Another triple album from George! This time it's the live recording of the famous concert of August 1971. Packaged in a luxurious box with booklet in which is reproduced the cheque handed over to the organisation helping the victims, and from which we learn that 44 microphones were used that day. It includes a rare performance by Bob Dylan, Ravi Shankar, Ringo, and a gentle acoustic interpretation of 'Here Comes The Sun'. It is a document of the last specks of dust of the Sixties.

WINGS OVER EUROPE

AFTER A SHORT, SPONTANEOUS AND UNADVERTISED TOUR OF ENGLISH UNIVERSITIES, WINGS LAUNCH THEIR EUROPEAN TOUR ON WHICH MUSICIANS, WIVES AND CHILDREN TRAVEL IN ONE SINGLE COLOURFUL BUS, REMINISCENT OF THE MAGICAL MYSTERY TOUR.

THE LYON CONCERT HAS TO BE CANCELLED FOR LACK OF TICKET SALES.

🥾🥾🥾🥾🤍

WINGS
Give Ireland back to the Irish

Single/February 72/Apple

- -

The first single from Wings is remarkable for being the first song by McCartney that is openly political. It was written in reaction to the famous Bloody Sunday massacre, in which 14 civil rights protesters were killed by the British Army.

The title was, of course, banned from the British airwaves, but reached number one in Ireland.

LIVE!

August 1972:
John Lennon at
Madison Square Garden
with Yoko and Elephant's
Memory for four charity
concerts, filmed for the
ABC TV channel with
Stevie Wonder and
Roberta Flack as
support acts.
There are also a
few guests like
Fred Astaire,
Andy Warhol
and George Harrison.

JOHN & YOKO / PLASTIC ONO BAND WITH ELEPHANT MEMORY
Some time in New York City

2 x LP/June 72/Apple

Engaged art. Huge debate. Lennon had the right to focus his ten new songs on "hot" political themes (feminism, John Sinclair, Bloody Sunday...). Unfortunately, the literal meaning of the words clashes with Spector's production and the extreme heaviness of the group Elephant's Memory, recruited to boost the Plastic Ono Band. Or more likely to crush it.

Some Time... struggled to number 48 in the American charts, which upset John Lennon enormously.

BORN TO BOOGIE

One year after its inauguration, Ringo has the new and shiny Studio Apple broken down and installs a film editing suite in its place.

Wings
Hi, Hi, Hi/C Moon

Single/December 72/Apple

Wings join the sparkly world of loudmouth, moronic glam-boogie. A title banned by the BBC for its alleged allusion to drugs, it was actually about sex (which would also have earned a ban). The vaguely reggae B-side is irritating, except for a bold bridge that almost saves it. In response to the ban, in May Wings release 'Mary Had A Little Lamb' which is deliberately banal.

RINGO STARR
Back off Boogaloo / Blindman

Single/March 72/Apple

A heartening A-side, inspired by his mate Marc Bolan, which resulted in an interesting promo video in which Ringo dances with Frankenstein's monster. And a surprising B-side with layers of futuristic synthesizer, Wendy Carlos fashion, and a finale in Johnny Cash style.

All in all, Ringo's best single.

73 John

appeals against the federal injunction ordering him to leave the USA within 60 days. His fight to remain in the USA is far from over. With Yoko, he moves into a luxurious duplex in the Dakota, an apartment building of Hanseatic Renaissance style that was built on Central Park West between 1880 and 1884.

RED & BLUE

IN APRIL, THOSE TWO DOUBLE ALBUMS COLLECT TOGETHER THE BEST BEATLES SONGS AND ARE HUGELY SUCCESSFUL. A NEW GENERATION DISCOVERS THE BAND AND GENERATES A SECOND POSTHUMOUS BEATLEMANIA.

That'll be the day

Ringo revisits his youth in this very Fifties film.

Paul McCartney & Wings
Red Rose Speedway

LP/May 73/Apple

On this album, which was originally planned as a double, McCartney enters the spirit of the Seventies with a Pink Floyd-like instrumental and titles that pre-empt Queen's A Night At The Opera, or which are reminiscent of the mainstream sound of Elton John in his good years. It's still full of delicious melodies ('Single Pigeon') and ballads languorously sweetened ('My Love'). There is even a second 'Hold Me Tight', albeit a different from the one on With The Beatles. In contrast, the medley ending side two is not very exciting, and the album seems sometimes to be on automatic pilot, lacking the nerve to be a total success.

James Paul McCartney

ANTI-LINDA!!!

Linda McCartney (on keyboards and unsteady backing vocals) within Wings is even more hated by Beatle fans than Yoko. She is accused of being responsible for "softening" Paul. And for preventing a hypothetical reformation of the "Four thirty-something lads".

PAUL McCARTNEY & WINGS
Live and let die / I lie around

Single/June 73/Apple

- - - - - - - - - - - - - - - - - - - -

Paul fulfils his contract for the soundtrack song of the new James Bond film.
A spectacular song, huge, almost monstrous, orchestrated by George Martin, with whom Paul hadn't worked for four years.

Liverpool 27/05/73: demolition of the original Cavern. The club is moved to the other side of the street. Since 1966, the Cavern has been struggling to survive. The stage on which the Beatles had played was destroyed and sold bit by bit to fans.

George Harrison
Living In The Material World

LP/June 73/Apple

- - - - - - - - - - - - - - - - - - - -

George is the only one of the four to have enjoyed anything like The Beatles' level of success since the split. This album, one of the few recorded in the short-lived Apple Studios, bears witness to his difficult return to earth. The atmosphere is melancholic and his voice more and more plaintive. And even the good tracks ('Give Me Love', 'Don't Let Me Wait Too Long') bring about some cosmic yawns here and there. A beautiful album nevertheless, replacing Red Rose Speedway at number one in the charts!

JOHN LENNON
Mind games

LP/June 73/Apple

- - - - - - - - - - - - - - - - - - - -

Pupil Lennon has shown in this last decade a certain disposition for learning. But we notice a drop this last term. John seems less motivated, doesn't apply himself the same way to his work and even his presentation appears lacking. Without being really bad, his recent homework is not very exciting, except for the very beautiful title-song. But, being indulgent, we haven't punished him for the crass verses he scratched on his desk, like 'Tight Ass' and 'Fuck Pig'.

John will have to pull himself together next term and stop living on past achievements.

- - - - - - - - - - - - - - - - - - - -

NUTOPIA!

John and Yoko announce the creation of a new conceptual country whose official anthem (six seconds of silence) is on *Mind Games.* *Nutopian Embassy One White Street NYC 10012*

Greetings from Lagos

On the point of leaving for Nigeria to record Wings' new album, Henry McCullough and Denny Seiwell quit the band. Never mind, Paul, Linda, Denny Laine and the engineer Geoff Emerick leave for Africa. But the little British gang who are dreaming of sun and coconuts discover, to their alarm, that Lagos is a huge and dangerous shantytown.

THE STUDIO IS MEDIOCRE. SOME OF THEIR MATERIAL IS STOLEN. PAUL DOESN'T FEEL WELL AT ALL. IN SPITE OF EVERYTHING, MOST OF THE ALBUM IS RECORDED IN LAGOS. DENNY PLAYS GUITAR AND PAUL DOES THE REST.

RINGO STARR
Ringo

LP/November 73/Apple

For his first solo album of unreleased songs, Ringo has asked for a little help from his friends. And among them are George Harrison, John Lennon and Paul McCartney. The four Beatles on the same record? Yes, but never at the same time, sadly.

A rather nice record, though one doesn't have the urge to get up in the middle of the night to listen to it.

Fela

The king of Afro-beat invites Paul into one of his clubs. Armed and threatening, he accuses Paul of coming to pillage African music. The meeting is stormy, but Fela listens to the tapes and admits his mistake.

PAUL McCARTNEY & WINGS
Band on the run

LP/December 73/Apple

The album, completed in London, is an immediate worldwide success, which surprises Paul. Considered dated from the beginning of Wings, he savours his return to the top. The public is not mistaken: Band On The Run, despite being recorded in pretty basic conditions, is nice work indeed. It's an ambitious record, crammed with well-written and well-produced songs, with a final medley, Paul McCartney's trademark since Abbey Road. And to reassure Fela Kuti, except for 'Mamounia' if that, there's nothing African on the horizon, which is perhaps a shame. Paul considered this record both "not African" and "very African" in its energy and dynamics.

"Exceptionally good work," says John Lennon, not normally given to generosity in his compliments towards Paul!

PAUL McCARTNEY & WINGS
Helen Wheels / Country dreamer

SP/October 73/Apple

LOST WEEKEND

In October, their relationship rocky, Yoko asks
John to leave New York with May Pang, their
secretary, to have fun and work on his problem
with alcohol. They settle in Los Angeles, where
a binge that will last for months starts.
Drunk, he records an album of old rock covers
with Spector, who fires a revolver in the studio. When John goes to retrieve the tapes,
Spector has already run off with them.

"THE LEAST YOU COULD CALL HIM IS ECCENTRIC,
AND THAT'S COMING FROM SOMEBODY WHO'S BARMY." -
John Lennon

HAMBURG'S SPIRIT?

Lennon, who cannot hold his drink, consumes alcohol excessively in LA with his friends Harry Nilsson and Ringo, the Hollywood Vampires. At the Troubadour, on March 12, he gets into a fight with the Smothers Brothers. He also wanders into the club with a sanitary pad stuck to his forehead. Photographers are present. John phones Yoko up to 20 times a day. But she believes he is "not ready".

Julian, 11 years old, comes to spend the holidays with his father in LA. He even plays the drums on the last track of the new album!

LOST WEEK END (2)

PUSSYCATS

John meets up with Paul when he comes to the beach-side house John is renting to record Nilsson's album Pussycats. Paul, by the edge of the swimming pool, has a message from Yoko to John. He can come back. But he will have to court her again in order to win her over.

That night, the two ex-Beatles jam with Stevie Wonder, Harry Nilsson and a mountain of coke.

RINGO STARR
Goodnight Vienna

LP/November 74/Apple

- -

The photo for the sleeve is based on the sci-fi cult movie The Day The Earth Stood Still by Robert Wise, dating from 1951. The expression "Goodnight Vienna" comes from a light opera from the Thirties that could be translated as "That's enough" or "That's about it". Example: "I had something else to say about that record, but I can't remember what. And Goodnight Vienna."

John Lennon. June 1952. AGE 11

Walls and Bridges

Football

As he wrote in the booklet for his album, on the August 23, 1974, John, naked on his balcony, sees a UFO. He calls May Pang, but she sees nothing. Obsessed by the vision, he immediately takes out a subscription to the magazine Flying Saucer Review.

On October 30, John poses for Bob Gruen.

In November, Allen Klein having lost his lawsuit, Paul, George and Ringo fly to the USA to sign the definitive agreement to end the partnership between the four musicians. But John refuses to leave his bed, "the stars not being favourable".

JOHN LENNON
Walls & bridges

LP/September 74/Apple

That's not right.

Ringo's album has sold three times more than Mind Games. Let's not even mention Band On The Run, the biggest seller by an ex-Beatle since Harrison's triple album. Lennon is cut to the quick.

Often associated with its predecessor, Walls & Bridges has nothing to do with Mind Games though. Funky and a bit greasy, influenced by the pre-disco sound of 1974, this record has amazing energy. It's the soundtrack to John's west coast drink binge, while Mind Games rather anticipated the hangover that followed.

There is a comedy, a song about his fear of getting old, one about his new enemy Allen Klein (with the violins of 'How Do You Sleep', well well...), and the moving and relevant 'Nobody Loves You (When You Are Down And Out)', that he would have liked to see interpreted by Sinatra!

And there's something strange at the end, a quick cover of 'Ya Ya' demo-style, randomly sung by John with a very young Julian on drums. The joke vexed the young boy. "You shouldn't have put it on the record," he allegedly said to his father, "I can play better than that."

The father-son relationship is obviously difficult for the Lennons.

Listen To This Ad.

"Whatever Gets You Thru' The Night"
John Lennon

MEET THE **RESIDENTS**
The first album by North Louisiana's Phenomenal Pop combo

Is it me or does it sound like?

- 'L'homme de ma Vie' by Diane Dufresne like Macca's 'Man We Was Lonely'
- 'J'ai Dix Ans' by Souchon like 'Bip Bop' by Wings
- 'Love Is All' by Roger Glover like 'Strawberry Fields'

🎵🎵🎵🎵🎵

PAUL McCARTNEY & WINGS
Junior's farm / Sally G.

Single/October 73/Apple

- -

🎵🎵🎵🎵🎵

THE COUNTRY HAMS
Walking in the park with Eloise

Single/October 74/EMI

Paul's non-album singles follow one another as in the Beatles great period. Here are two new ones, issued simultaneously. The first is classic Wings, the second more surprising. It's also by Wings plus Chet Atkins and Floyd Kramer using a pseudonym. They interpret this tasty Charleston, an old composition by Jim, Paul's father!

George creates his own label, Dark Horse. His own studio, the "F.P.S.H.O.T." is operational in a wing of his Friar Park mansion in Henley-on-Thames.

John Lennon's last concert.

Elton John had advised John Lennon to beef up the tempo of the single 'Whatever Gets You Thru The Night'.

Lennon had promised Elton he would go on stage with him if the single reached number one. And it did.

On November 28, suffering his usual stage fright, the ex-Beatle goes on stage at New York's Madison Square Garden and sings three songs, among them 'I Saw Her Standing There' that he introduces as a song written "with an old estranged fiancée of mine named Paul."

dark year

Pattie has left with his mate Eric Clapton. George goes on a big American tour, his first, but problems with his voice sabotage most dates. In San Francisco, Paul & Linda, wearing wigs, attend, incognito, the concert by the hoarse guitarist.

🎵🎵🎵🎵🎵

GEORGE HARRISON
Dark Horse

LP/December 74/Apple

- -

After John, George also chooses a "nostalgic" sleeve: his class photo from the Fifties, revisited ashram-style. There's a nostalgic feel to the record too. Although the album as a whole has more go than his previous one, there is a big problem. Harrison, suffering from laryngitis, sings abominably. That's the reason why the critics have re-named that album "Dark Hoarse". And the last title, in the mode of 'The Inner Light' but in boogaloo, is a joke, right?

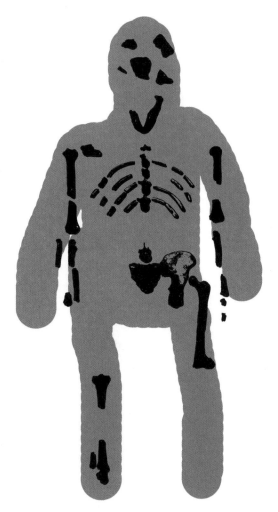

On November 28, 1974, the oldest fossil
of a hominid ever discovered is unearthed
by Yves Coppens' team. At that moment,
'Lucy In The Sky With Diamonds' was
playing on the radio. The fossil is named
"LUCY".

75 LOST WEEK-END (END)

Yoko comes to speak to John backstage after the concert with Elton John. Soon after, John is allowed to return to live with his wife at the Dakota, 18 months after being banished. *The separation failed.*

January 1975. A judge rules that the entity Beatles is "officially dissolved". On the 26th, **the contract with EMI expires. Apple's** offices close down.

JOHN LENNON
Rock'n'roll

LP/February 75/Apple

For a long time John has wanted to record some rock classics, and an album like this would help him lose the "Come together/ You can't catch me" allegation of plagiarism. Unfortunately, two years after American Graffiti and the first version of Rock'n'roll with whisky and Spector, the Fifties revival has all but petered out. Especially since these sincere but slightly labouring covers don't really improve on the excellent (and seminal) original recordings.

It has often been said that Lennon was the rocker in the Beatles. It's still the case, but he's a rocker grown slightly too comfortable.

RINGO GETS A DIVORCE AND PLAYS THE POPE IN LISZTOMANIA.

The Grammy Awards, John & Yoko's first outing since their reconciliation. Everybody admires Yoko's round tummy.

Elvis

LENNON + BOWIE = FAME!

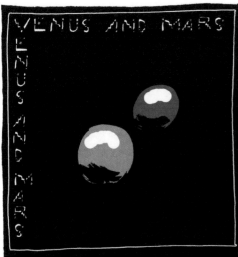

VENUS AND MARS

WINGS
Venus and mars

LP/May 75/EMI

First post-Apple record (sniff) for Paul. Since **Band On The Run**, he is no longer an ex-Beatle but the leader of Wings, one of the most famous bands of the era, especially in the USA. Less inspired than the previous album, Venus And Mars, recorded in New Orleans, sounds more adult, more American, but doesn't reflect the city in which it was created. Conceived to be performed during a tour of the States that has just been announced, its first side is good but it takes a turn for the worse on side two, Paul having had the strange idea of introducing democracy to the band. A shame, for Denny Laine and Jimmy McCullough's titles are crap, there is no other way to say it.

To celebrate the end of the recording of *Venus And Mars*, EMI organises a cocktail party at Long Beach, on the cruiser the *Queen Mary*. A few guests from this most mythical party of the Seventies: Michael Jackson, Dylan, Bowie, Marvin Gaye, Led Zep... and George Harrison who hasn't spoken to Paul since the split!

ROCKSHOW!

Raring to go, Paulo wants the Wings tour to be the biggest tour ever. High on the success of *Venus And Mars*, the band rehearse to perfection, and go from one gig to the next in England, before launching an attack on Australia. A real Wingsmania follows. And Paul begins to mix Beatles hits with those from Wings.

During a tribute show to Sir Lew Grade, the last televised appearance by John, he sings two songs in a boiler suit and slicked-back hair.

The day her husband turns 35, Yoko gives birth to Sean Taro Ono Lennon.

George Harrison

EXTRA TEXTURE

GEORGE HARRISON
Extra texture

LP/October 75/Apple

George is back to his mischievous self. On a photo in the booklet, the caption reads: "OHNOTHIMAGAIN", inspired by the fall-out with his audience dating from the pitiful year 1974. And on the label on this album recorded to end his contract with EMI-Apple, the apple has been chewed! Considered his worst album by its creator, it is easier on the ear than the previous one. And the voice is back.

MAL EVANS, the gentle giant, the Beatles' handyman, is shot dead by LA police after his girlfriend had called them during a marital dispute. Mal had pointed an air gun at the policemen.

Father McKenzie

By a strange coincidence, John and Paul lose their fathers in the space of a few days. James 'Jim' McCartney dies of pneumonia, aged 74. He has remained close to his son.

Alfred 'Freddy' Lennon dies of cancer, aged 64. John had phoned him several times during his last few weeks.

DAKOTA 76

Paul and John are eating pizzas in front of the TV at the Dakota when the possibility of a Beatles reunion is mentioned on the show Saturday Night Live. They decide to call a taxi and go to the studios to make a surprise appearance. Then they open some beer cans and forget the whole thing.

WINGS
Wings at the speed of sound

LP/March 76/EMI

- -

WINGS
Wings over America

LP/December 76/EMI

- -

Before addressing the flaws, let's mention the gold nugget on *Wings At The Speed Of Sound*, an album recorded during Wings' big tour: the last song, 'Warm And Beautiful', somewhere between Brian Wilson's 'Surf's Up' and an-Irish-song-that-makes-you-sob-in-your-beer.

The rest is rather hideous, and it's a Macca fan speaking. Again, as democracy demands, four titles out of 11 are composed and sung by the other members of the band, and one title is sung by Linda. Five songs remain for Paul, off form, except for the sublime final number. It has been suggested that the Peter Frampton-Elton John-Wings decadent rock-business with its ever-growing mainstream albums, overproduced and complacent, justified the success of (and the need for) punk this year, 1976. Listening to this record is enough to convince anyone.

By comparison, the triple live album released for Christmas and celebrating the tour is pretty good.

"It's good to be legal again."

On June 27, after a five year legal battle, John Lennon obtains his Green Card. In 1981 he will even be able to apply for American citizenship.

The New York punk band has taken its name as a tribute to McCartney's pseudonym in 1960, Paul Ramon. "Ram on" is also the title of a song on his album "RAM".

GEORGE HARRISON
Thirty three & 1/3

LP/November 76/Dark Horse

George is still dogged by bad luck. Ill with hepatitis, the recording of his new album suffers delays and because his label Dark Horse is not successful, he is forced to end his contract with A&M and join Warners. Despite it all, this very autobiographical album ("33 & 1/3" is the rotation speed of a vinyl LP and Harrison's age in 76) breaks the series of very average albums by our man who's in better form here. Unfortunately, for all that, it is not indispensable. Sales were considered insufficient. But a flop with 800,000 copies sold would make many acts perfectly happy!

The single 'This Song' relates to his lost trial for plagiarism (see 1971).

The Chiffons ended up covering 'My Sweet Lord' in 1975!

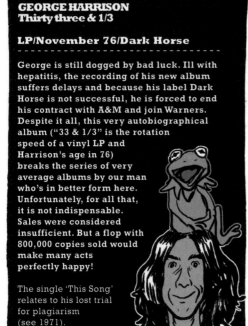

Ringo Starr
Ringo's Rotogravure

LP/September 76/Polydor

Rotogravure is the other name for heliography, a clever printing technique used for very big editions like the printing of stamps. Indeed, its copper cylinder (or stainless steel sometimes) is unbreakable and allows for a good quality of screen.

"One day I'll be 95, I'll be in a wheelchair (...) and people will say: 'Ah! An ex-Beatle'."
(RINGO, interviewed by Philippe Manoeuvre in *Rock&Folk*, November 1976).

House-husband

John Lennon hasn't sought a new record contract at the end of the deal that bound him to EMI for 14 years. He has decided to drop music and devote himself exclusively to his baby son Sean, while Yoko takes charge of the business.

77

The Clash — 1977 / WHITE RIOT

NO ELVIS, BEATLES OR ROLLING STONES IN 1977!

If the Beatles from the Hamburg period were punks without knowing it, 1977 is the year the ex-Fab Four have become passé to a new generation.

Ten years after *Sgt Pepper*, the world has changed a lot.

THE BEATLES AT THE HOLLYWOOD BOWL

The Beatles' sons?

They have carried the torch from where the Beatles stopped, at the end of the *Abbey Road* medley.

But Electric Light Orchestra and Supertramp share the same flaws. They are professional but dull. They are Beatles without rock. They rely too heavily on virtuosity and production techniques which their inspiration never needed.

It makes us shudder to think what the Beatles might have produced if they hadn't split.

Even the sleeve of the latest Supertramp is reminiscent of the film HELP!

THE BEATLES
The Beatles at the Hollywood Bowl

LP/May 77/Parlophone

- -

Now we can say it loud, the Beatles concerts were a rip-off. Not those at the Star-Club, Lennon himself said the stage peak of the band was in Hamburg. Not the mythical shows at the Cavern, or the 1963 English tour either. We're talking here about the Beatlemania concerts, from 1964-66. Imagine the scene. Stadiums or gymnasiums with a sound system thrown together. Girls screaming like banshees. Ringo always marking the same tempo. Nobody can hear a bloody thing. Nobody can see a bloody thing. After a 25 minutes show, the musicians run off, relieved not to have been bumped off by a KKK sniper.

However, it was perfect. Exciting. Unique. And this document perfectly reflects a typical concert of that blessed period. Special mention from this live recording from 1964 and '65 goes to 'Things We Said Today', performed in a particularly punchy and surprising fashion.

Quiet verses. Powerful choruses.
Nirvana or the Pixies?

- -

12/09 BIRTH OF JAMES McCARTNEY, PAUL'S FIRST SON AND HIS THIRD CHILD.

PASTICHE BY NATIONAL LAMPOON

Magic Alex, Apple's ex-electro wiz is now security consultant for the Sultan of Oman.

THE BEATLES Live! at the Star-Club in Hamburg, Germany; 1962.

THE BEATLES
Live ! At the Star-Club in Hamburg, Germany; 1962

2xLP/April 77/Lingasong

The Beatles Live at Hamburg' Star-Club! It must have been quite something! Well, it doesn't come across here to be honest, for the sound on this double album seems like a dirty old bootleg recorded on a home reel-to-reel tape recorder. It will be called an "interesting document", from which we note that the repertoire of those young Liverpudlian punks would later become very famous. 'Twist And Shout', 'I Saw Her Standing There', 'Long Tall Sally' and 'Ask Me Why' are already in place.

The tapes from this show were offered, at too high a price, to Brian Epstein, then to George Harrison, also unsuccessfully. The ex-Beatles even attempted to prevent the release of the recording, but all in vain. In April 1977, the label Lingasong distributes it worldwide.

The original tape was made by Ted Taylor of Kingsize Taylor & The Dominoes. John Lennon had allowed him to record the show in exchange for a few beers...

Return of *Beatles Book Monthly*, and the first issue of Club Sandwich, Paul McCartney's "Fun Club".

Domestic Johnny

Between baking homemade bread, of which he is particularly proud, and changing Sean's nappies, John records the demos of the songs 'Free As A Bird' and 'Real Love'.

Ringo Starr
Ringo The Fourth

LP/September 77/Polydor

This Ringo disco doesn't even enter the charts.

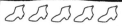

Wings
Mull Of Kintyre/Girl's School

Single/November 77/Polydor

Save the lambs, spare their bellies! Boycott the pipes and this aberrant single! Fake traditional Scottish song composed by Macca, 'Mull Of Kintyre' sells three million copies in one month in the UK alone, making it the most popular single of all time, eclipsing 'She Loves You'.

On the first album of the young Björk Gudmundsdottír (11 years old), there's a cover of 'The Fool On The Hill', renamed here "Alfur 'ut 'uh hot".

78

The ex-Beatles

sue the company Apple Computers, created in 1976 by Steve Jobs and two associates for fraudulent use of their name. Apple Corps, the Beatles company, is no longer active, but the name is registered. An agreement is reached a few months later for a substantial sum and a promise that Apple Computers will not become involved with music. In exchange, Apple Corps promises not to manufacture computers. That's a shame, Magic Alex could have been put back to work.

WINGS
London Town

LP/March 78/EMI

After Scotland, London, Lagos and New Orleans, Wings record on a yacht in the Virgin Islands! And here we go again, as with *Band On The Run*, Paul, Linda and Denny end up as three, Joe English and Jimmy McCullough having "abandoned ship". There are clearly personnel problems in that band...

Less catastrophic than At *The Speed Of Sound*, London Town, when it turns to rockabilly ('Name And Address'), or epic disco ('Morse Moose...') is even exciting. But a good half of the album is poor. As for 'With A Little Luck', the album's single, it inaugurates Paul McCartney's new style of synthetic pop, a bit soul, a bit bland, ready for the international charts of the eighties which are looming on the horizon.

Pistols gob on USA
Siouxsie/Boz Scaggs
Groovies/ Rods tour

Oh no, not another
punk on the cover!

Yeah, just another angry working-class
kid in black leather, destined for
God-knows-where. Which reminds us,
where the hell are you, John Lennon?

THE RUTLES
ALL YOU NEED IS CASH

Created by former members of Monty Python and the Bonzo Dog Doo Dah Band, this hilarious spoof documentary recounts the career of the Rutles, a Sixties band from the tiny county of Rutland. It's all there: the Cavern, Rutlemania, their "tea" consumption, their label (whose symbol is a banana)... Mick Jagger and George Harrison, who loves it, make an appearance. There are impeccable pastiches, an LP and a single are released. The song 'Cheese And Onion' even ends up on a Beatles bootleg as an unreleased 1968 song!

The typical bad good idea.
A hideous film in which the Bee Gees, Peter Frampton, Billy Preston and many others perform disco/pop versions of Beatles songs. A flop, except in Poland, where a million cinemagoers are counted...

George Harrison,

like John Lennon, seems tired of showbiz. He marries Olivia Arias, a secretary at his label Dark Horse. On the first of August, a little boy, Dhani, is born.

The punk band from Lyon releases a single disparaging the Fab-Four called 'ON VEUT PLUS DES BEATLES ET D'LEUR MUSIQUE DE MERDE' ('WE NO LONGER WANT THE BEATLES AND THEIR SHITTY MUSIC').

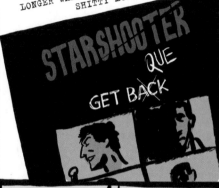

RINGO STARR
Bad boy

LP/April 78/Polydor

...Or the ravages of alcoholism.

KARUIZAWA

John, finally able to leave the USA without risking problems on his return, leaves with wife and son for Japan. Yoko introduces him to her family and John and Sean discover the land of her ancestors. On photographs taken there John looks serene, appeased.
In a word, Zen.

Yoko invests!
She buys rare antiques, luxurious houses and hundreds of acres in Delaware for her prize cows to graze on.

79

"A love letter from John & Yoko, to people to ask us what, when and why"

an incomprehensible advertisement that appears in the New York Times on May 27.

George Harrison

For the first time in his career, Paul is refused the EMI studios because another artist is recording there. Never mind, McCartney has the exact copy of Studio 2 Abbey Road built in London that he calls "Replica studio". *Back To The Egg* is recorded there.

🐾🐾🐾🐾🐾

WINGS
Back to the egg

LP/June 79/EMI

- -

The first four songs are very good ('Getting Closer' is smashing, and on 'Reception' his bass playing is fashioned on Chic's 'Good Times'), the last three titles too. It's in between that it takes a turn for the worse, the soft underbelly of that album being very soft and very pot-bellied. The best songs have a new wave energy about them, but the poorer titles evoke rather awkward, hard FM synthetics. A shame.

- -

🐾🐾🐾🐾🐾

GEORGE HARRISON
George Harrison

LP/February 79/Dark Horse

- -

George Harrison is a typical old hippie. He surely doesn't give a damn about the Sex Pistols and his new album is like his previous ones. Some beautiful songs, others rather boring and conventional, all at an average tempo. Even his single 'Faster', a tribute to the Formula One racing that he adores, runs at only 50 kilometres an hour.

Note the presence of 'Not Guilty', the cursed song from the White Album, that he has finally managed to finish 11 years later.

In 1979, George drives high-powered cars, throws himself into cinema production and has a jam with Ringo and Paul at the party to celebrate Pattie's marriage to Eric Clapton!

WINGS
Goodnight tonight / Daytime...

Single/March 79/EMI

- -

John Lennon says of this disco hit that he isn't much impressed by the song but that Paul's bass line was extremely enjoyable. Well summed up.

The promoter Sid Bernstein unsuccessfully offers $500 million to the ex-Beatles for a reunion concert!

Mark Chapman, 24 years old, settles in Waikiki and marries a Hawaiian woman of Japanese origin, like his hero John Lennon. Depressed, Chapman becomes violent and alcoholic.

ANNUS HORRIBILIS

Ringo escapes death by the skin of his teeth after a fire at his Hollywood home but the Beatles memorabilia he had accumulated over the years goes up in smoke.

Allen Klein spends two months in jail for not declaring his income on the sale of promo records in 1970-1972. Among them, the Bangladesh Concert charity album!

Classy!

Jimmy McCullough, guitarist with Wings between 1974 and 77, takes a fatal overdose. He had composed two anti-drug songs for the band...

WONDERFUL CHRISTMASTIME

PAUL McCARTNEY

RHODIUM

The Guinness Book of Records offers Paul a rhodium record symbolising the millions of records sold by him since 1962. The biggest vinyl seller of all time.

John & Yoko

offer $1,000 towards equipping New York policemen with bullet-proof jackets.

1980

PAUL IN JAIL!

Wings undertake a soldout tour of Japan, 14 years after the Beatles! Unfortunately, as soon as he arrives at the airport, Paul is arrested for possession of marijuana (210 grams). He spends 10 days in prison and the tour is cancelled.

McCARTNEY II

March

For their 11th wedding anniversary, John offers Yoko a diamond heart, and Yoko offers John a vintage Rolls.

SOUND AFFECTS

PAUL McCARTNEY
McCartney II

LP/May80/Emi

- -

How old is that young man on the sleeve? 23? 28? No, he's 38 and doesn't seem to want to grow old yet.

While testing his new Scottish home-studio, Paul McCartney has written an album, a necessary relaxation after the stress in Japan. Like he did 10 years before, on his first solo album, Paul has done everything alone. Though some feel it's complacent, the ex-Beatle impresses with his Stakhanovism and taste for revitalisation and experimentation, which he doesn't share with his ex-colleagues...

Will this album, sometimes stupid, sometimes fun and sometimes glorious, be a new departure for Macca, the Dorian Gray of Pop?

- -

ROCK LOBSTER* !

THE JOHNANDYOKO RELATIONSHIP IS SHAKY AGAIN. JOHN LEAVES FOR BERMUDA ON A YACHT. IN A CLUB, HE HEARS THIS SONG BY THE B52'S AND IT'S A SHOCK TO HIS SYSTEM. HE HAD ALSO LIKED McCARTNEY II. HE CALLS YOKO IMMEDIATELY: "GET THE AXE OUT — THEY'RE READY FOR US AGAIN!"

HE GOES BACK TO COMPOSING STRAIGHT AWAY.

Return on investment

A Regis Holstein cow from the Lennons' livestock is sold for $264 000 at a show.

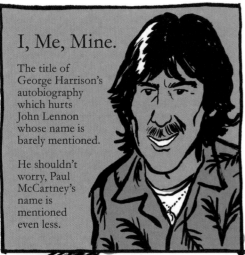

I, Me, Mine.

The title of George Harrison's autobiography which hurts John Lennon whose name is barely mentioned.

He shouldn't worry, Paul McCartney's name is mentioned even less.

On October 27 Mark Chapman buys a .38 gun. Obsessed by Lennon and JD Salinger's The Catcher In The Rye, he increases his trips back and forth between Hawaii and New York.

The series of photos taken by Annie Leibovitz, 8/12/80.

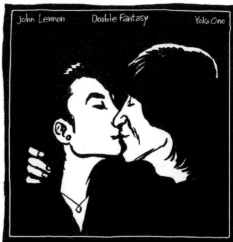

John Lennon   Double Fantasy   Yoko Ono

JOHN LENNON & YOKO ONO
Double fantasy

LP/November 80/Geffen

Contrary to Paul, who seems to have a mental age of eight on his last album, John Lennon accepts his age on the comeback album he shares with Yoko. It's soft rock for the over forties. The production is square, slightly clinical, formatted for 1980's US radio. It's good to hear that voice again, absent from vinyl for six years. Some of Yoko's titles are pleasing, like the new wave-ska 'Kiss Kiss Kiss', which reminds us that her 10-year-old album *Fly* was way in advance of its time. "It's just like starting over," says John in the lovely opening song on the record. Let's hope the next album he has already planned will be a tad more daring. And that he will sing more than six tracks this time!

(JUST LIKE) STARTING OVER

After five years looking after his son, John is brimming with energy and projects. In Bermuda he composes nearly 25 songs and, in the summer, over three weeks, a new album by John and Yoko is recorded, while a second, called *Milk And Honey*, is planned for 1981. John & Yoko sign with Geffen Records, the brand new label formed by David Geffen, which takes everybody by surprise.

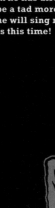

Life begins at 40

After spending the Seventies feeling old (like all thirty-something rockers) John is feeling good for the first time in his life. Serene, relaxed. He has a haircut at the beginning of December, fashioned on himself circa Hamburg 1960... That was 20 years ago.

On December 6, Mark Chapman is back in New York. Suffering from hallucinations, he sees Lennon as the cause of all his problems.

The hero of his youth, the hippie idealist with glasses, has, according to him, become a cynical and selfish multi-millionaire, deceiving a whole generation of fans who believed he was going to save the world.

PLAYBOY

In a long and flowing interview given to David Sheff at the Dakota, John goes back over his life: lucid, witty and at times moving. Relaxed, drinking tea and smoking Gitanes, he even gives his opinion on many Beatle songs.

On December 8, at 3p.m., Chapman, in the entrance hall of the Dakota, offers a copy of Double Fantasy to Lennon to sign before he leaves with Yoko for the Record Plant studio where they work on their next album.

At 10.49 p.m., they are back at the Dakota. Chapman, who has been waiting for hours in the street, takes out his gun and shoots John Lennon five times.

The police intervene quickly, Chapman offers no resistance.

At 11.07p.m., John Lennon is declared dead.

1940-1980

Fans are distraught when they hear about the death of their idol.
Paul McCartney, in a state of shock, is lost for words and can only
mutter "It's a drag" when approached by reporters.

The day after, a huge crowd assembles around the Dakota. The
following Sunday, in New York, London, Liverpool and elsewhere,
fans observe a 10 minute silence.

John Lennon is cremated.
No one knows
what Yoko Ono
has done with the ashes.

81

"Will I be the next?"

wonder the remaining Beatles who drastically reassess their security systems. Ringo leaves the USA for Monaco where he feels safer.

In April, the three men gather for the wedding of the bearded drummer to the ex-James Bond girl Barbara Bach.

On August 20, 1981 Mark Chapman is sentenced to life imprisonment with a minimum of twenty years. He hasn't pleaded insanity.

*George Harrison
Somewhere in England*

**GEORGE HARRISON
Somewhere in England**

LP/June 81/Dark Horse

Mortified that his autobiography (see 1980) offended John before his death, Harrison rewrites his nostalgic song 'All Those Years Ago' as a dedication to John. A real transatlantic hit with Ringo on drums and Paul & Linda doing backing vocals. It's the only great song on this album, which to be honest cannot be considered a major work in twentieth century music.

Considered by the New Musical Express the worse record of 1981.

Roxy Music reach number one for the first and only time with a cover of 'Jealous Guy', a tribute to John Lennon.

Exit Wings

After the Japanese fiasco and Paul's solo album, Wings abandon recording their new album *Cold Cuts* on December 8, after the death of John. At the beginning of 1981, McCartney announces he is recording a solo album in Montserrat with George Martin, Stevie Wonder and the young prodigy Michael Jackson, with whom he writes songs and becomes friends. In April, Denny Laine announces he is leaving Wings.

RINGO IN THE PREHISTORIC TURKEY CAVEMAN

Grammy

Huge emotion during the Grammy Awards when Yoko and Sean come to collect their award for *Double Fantasy*.

PAUL McCARTNEY

TUG OF WAR

Da, da, da

Klaus Voorman, their friend from Hamburg, designer of the *Revolver* cover and Lennon's bass player, produces this annoying international hit.

BEATLESONGS!

RHINO RECORDS HAS TO WITHDRAW THIS COMPILATION FROM THE SHOPS. ON ITS SLEEVE, THE ARTIST WILLIAM STOUT HAS DRAWN MARK CHAPMAN AMONG FANS AT A BEATLES CONVENTION.

WE LOVE YOU BEATLES

George Harrison
Gone Troppo

LP/November 82/Dark horse

In the era of new wave, post-punk and the beginning of hip-hop, rare are the children of the Sixties who still release decent records. Even the incredible sleeve of Gone Troppo ("gone mad" in Australia) suggests that listening to this album will prove tedious. The presence of 'Circles', a song originally composed for the White Album, doesn't prevent a flop. Having lost the taste for music and the music business itself, George is nowadays involved in film production.

Paul McCartney
Tug of war

LP/April 82/EMI

In France, we don't do rock, but we do French baguette. And like rock, a good baguette is about know-how. A balance. The crust must be golden, which gives it its crispiness, obviously. And the dough must be both light and firm, that gives it its softness. Well, with the album Tug Of War, Macca the baker forgets the formula. He tries both to evoke the spirit of the Beatles (George Martin, Geoff Emerick at the desk, a little bit of 'Let It Be' in 'Here Today' as a tribute to John) and jump on the 1982 pop bandwagon. Of course it is successful and sells millions. 'Ebony And Ivory' with Stevie Wonder makes a hell of a hit.

But there is too much dough.

George Martin is hilarious in the video promo for 'Take It Away', grooving behind his keyboard like a man possessed.

Michael & Paul

Much has happened since their 1981 recordings. In the meantime, Michael Jackson has become the biggest pop phenomenon since the Beatles! He and Paul have recorded four songs, among them 'The Girl Is Mine' on *Thriller*, now well on its way to becoming the best selling album of all time.

Jackson admits the "crossover" style of pop and funk that he invented in 1982 came from his meeting with McCartney.

McCARTNEY & MICHAEL JACKSON
Say say say / Ode to a koala bear

PAUL McCARTNEY
Pipes of peace

Single + LP/October 83/Parlophone

'Say Say Aay' benefits from a pretty melody, Michael Jackson's vocal prowess is terrific, and it was a monster hit (the seventh number one for Jacko, we no longer keep count of Macca's). But it is also laboured and a bit twee. However, let's recognise Paul's prescience for recording with the new "king of pop" a few months before his massive success.

The album Pipes Of Peace is the logical follow-up to Tug Of War. We have now entered the least interesting period of Paul's career, one of comfortable but dubious choices.

AVAILABLE IN CANADA, IN MEXICO, JAPAN AND GERMANY, BUT NOT IN THE USA OR UK.

James Jameson, the bass player on many great Motown records and a key influence on Paul McCartney, passes away.

On January 12, the astronomer Brian Skaff discovers a new asteroid. It is given the number 4147 and is named "Lennon". Over the following six months, the asteroids 4148, 4149 and 4150 are discovered and named "McCartney", "Harrison" and "Starr", which makes perfect sense.

After Peter Ham in 1975, Tom Evans, another member of BADFINGER commits suicide. This cursed band was one of the most talented of the Seventies. Formerly the IVEYS, they had recorded four good albums for Apple between1969 and 73. Neil Aspinall named them after 'Bad Finger Boogie', the working title of 'With A Little Help From My Friends'.

84

JULIAN LENNON VALOTTE

JULIAN LENNON, 21, RELEASES HIS FIRST ALBUM, WHICH IS A SUCCESS. THE VOCAL AND PHYSICAL RESEMBLANCE TO HIS FATHER PLAYS A BIG PART IN IT. THE SINGLE 'VALOTTE' CERTAINLY WOULDN'T HAVE BEEN OUT OF PLACE ON DOUBLE FANTASY.

John Lennon   Milk and Honey   Yoko Ono

JOHN LENNON AND YOKO ONO
Milk and honey

LP/January 84/Polydor

Four years later, here are the demos of the album that John and Yoko were recording just before the assassination.
Was it a good idea to release these works-in-progress? The occasionally embarrassing material leads us to reply "no". Once finished, would Milk And Honey have been a good album? The answer: "We don't know." Nothing here makes us think so.

Paul, who has started painting, is the biggest collector of Magritte's paintings in the world. During an auction, Linda buys him the artist's easel and materials.

This is not a beetle.

In April, the city of Liverpool opens the first permanent exhibition devoted to the Beatles.

In November, Paul receives the medal of the city.

Video promo

The Beatles invented the concept as early as 1966 with small films to promote 'Paperback Writer' and 'Rain'. There were others too. The singles by Wings also had their little video promos, but the genre really became popular with the launch of specialised channels like MTV in 1981. Paul had just made a feature-length video called Give My Regards To Broad Street where, in an embarrassing sequence, he re-interprets 'Silly Love Songs' dressed as a neo-romantic clown with a hip-hop dancer.

On their return from Barbados, Linda is arrested at Heathrow Airport.

Guess why?

For possessing cannabis, of course!

85

$$$!

Paul McCartney, who owns, among other things, the publishing rights to Buddy Holly's songs, had advised Michael Jackson to invest the fortune earned through *Thriller* in buying up song publishing catalogues.

Michael Jackson did just that - he bought the Beatles songs!

He has acquired 100% of ATV Music, which owns Northern Songs, for $45.5 million.

Yoko and Paul, flabbergasted, tried to bid higher but in vain.

POPSTARS

like The Beatles. Jackson is sporting a very *Sgt Pepper's* jacket and Prince injects some psychedelics into his funk ('Around The World In A Day').

Ringo is the first Beatle to become a grand-dad! (Tatia Jayne Starkey, daughter of Zac).

Is it me or does it sound like? 'No Comment' by Gainsbourg like 'Say Say Say' (OUH OUH OUH)

Denny Laine is broke. He has to sell his rights on 'Mull of Kintyre', that he co-wrote with Paul.

In Central Park, Yoko inaugurates the Strawberry Fields Memorial, 10,000 square metres dedicated to the memory of John Lennon.

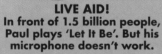

LIVE AID!
In front of 1.5 billion people, Paul plays 'Let It Be'. But his microphone doesn't work.

SESSIONS!

The fans have been waiting since 1970.

EMI prepares the release of the Sessions album, compiling a dozen unreleased tracks by the Beatles.

Unfortunately, Yoko and the three former members of the band block the album's release, feeling that a more ambitious, more "anthological" project would be preferable.

handmade *films*

Having financed the excellent *Life Of Brian* by Monty Python, George Harrison produces *Shanghai Surprise* with Madonna and Sean Penn.

A flop.

DEATH OF THE NIGERIAN MUSICIAN JIMMY SCOTT EMUAKPOR, WHOSE BAND OBLA-DI OBLA-DA HAD INFLUENCED PAUL MCCARTNEY TO WRITE THE SONG OF THE SAME NAME.

A SONG DESCRIBED AS "PAUL'S GRANNY SHIT" BY JOHN LENNON.

The mythical white Volkswagen from the Abbey Road sleeve is sold for £2,300 at Sotheby's.

PAUL McCARTNEY
Press to play

LP/September 86/Parlophone

For sure, this is Paul McCartney's worst album. It's not so much that the songs are bad. The problem is that the songs are lost beneath a multitude of trendy synthetic effects, all very irritating indeed. While Paul had been using technology in a playful and ingenious way on *McCartney II*, here he seems to have given in to it instead. The king of made-to-measure sound has converted to 1980s prêt-à-porter, like any new Top 50 one-hit wonder.

JOHN LENNON · MENLOVE AVENUE

JOHN LENNON
Live in New York city

LP/February 86/Parlophone

JOHN LENNON
Menlove avenue

LP/November 86/Parlophone

Lennon's heritage continues to be released. This live album, recorded on August 30, 1972, is agreeable, full of hits, even though the sound recording is not always brilliant. Yoko has been reproached for having chosen this first concert when the next day's was considered better. A VHS of this concert has also been released. *Menlove Avenue*, named after the road where John was raised, is a compilation of unreleased titles and demos from the 'Lost Weekend' period. The sleeve was designed by Andy Warhol.

Not bad, but still "for fans only".

Stella McCartney, Paul's 15-year-old daughter, is a gifted fashion designer. She helps produce Christian Lacroix's first haute couture collection.

87

This Is George!

On October 21, Paul, George and Ringo have dinner at a chic Chinese restaurant in St John's Wood. They end up at in Paul's Cavendish Avenue home, where they talk till dawn.

Paul spends an evening with Julian, explaining the origin of the song 'Hey Jude'.

hamlyn — EMI

The Complete **BEATLES** Recording Sessions

MARK LEWISOHN'S BOOK ON ALL THE BEATLES RECORDING SESSIONS!

"It was 20 years ago *today*"

On the 20th anniversary of its original release, *Sgt Pepper* is issued on CD and Paul attends a press reception at Abbey Road. The CD goes straight into the English charts at number three. From the middle of May 1988, all Beatles albums are finally available on CD.

GEORGE HARRISON
Cloud nine

LP/November 87/Dark horse

New balls! Five years after his last crime, *Gone Troppo*, George, who since then has been busy with movies, Formula 1 and tending the roses in the huge garden at his mansion, does a backhand with topspin style comeback. Accompanied by a few friends, he plays his best match since the triple *All Things Must Pass*. The slightly flashy but solid coaching of Jeff Lynne, ex-ELO, highlights some excellent compositions. George is in great shape, as shown on the sleeve, the weakest element of the album. Photos in the booklet show Eric Clapton and Elton John in tracksuits obviously enjoying playing tennis between takes. Or the other way around. More than one million copies of *Cloud Nine* are sold in the USA alone, and the excellent 'Got My Mind Set On You' (an obscure song by Rudy Clarke), 'This Is Love' and 'When We Was Fab' (very 'Walrus', with sleeve by Voorman as a wink to *Revolver*) are all amongst George's best late period songs.

> **Author' note: for my 14th birthday, my mother gave me a small book on the Beatles, designed like a single, written by Merle & Volcouve. It was the origin of an obsession.**

88

Ringo and Barbara battle their alcoholism detoxing in a Tucson clinic

THE BEATLES Past masters 1 & 2

2xLP/Mars 88/Parlophone

Two albums that gather all the Beatles singles unreleased on albums as well as their B-sides. What a brilliant idea.

The first record (black) runs from 'Love Me Do' to 'I'm Down', and includes the German versions of 'She Loves You' and 'I Want To Hold You hand', recorded at the height of Beatlemania.

The second (white) runs from 'Day Tripper' to 'You Know My Name...', the B-side of 'Let It Be', and includes all the singles from the mature years (except those from 1967, now available on *Magical Mystery Tour*).

These two records are not just an essential complement to the Beatles albums.

These are arguably the best Beatles albums.

The Wilbury brothers

Originally George, pushed for time, was only going to record a B-side with his hero Roy Orbison. But then he asked his friends Bob Dylan, Tom Petty and Jeff Lynne to join forces and conceive an album together!

The Slovenian band Laibach releases an album on which they good-naturedly cover the whole *Let It Be* album in industrial-totalitarian style.

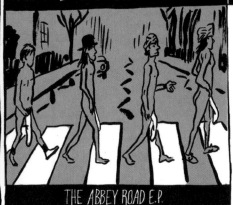

THE RED HOT CHILI PEPPERS

THE ABBEY ROAD E.P.

THE TRAVELING WILBURYS Vol. 1

LP/October 88/Wilbury records

A supergroup that gathers so many stars that at first we don't believe it. Then, we don't trust it. Supergroups are often super-disappointing.

So what makes this gathering of legends from the fifties and sixties work so well? We will never know, and it's not important. It is fresh and dynamic, the songs are good, nobody's taking over, and even Dylan sings decently. As for the great and humble Roy Orbison, after years of oblivion, this project puts him back in the place he should never have left. On top.

Saint John's hagiography is released into the cinemas in October 1988.

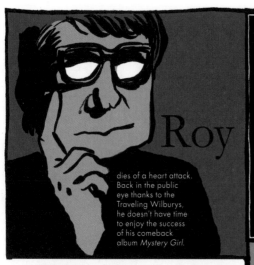

Roy dies of a heart attack. Back in the public eye thanks to the Traveling Wilburys, he doesn't have time to enjoy the success of his comeback album *Mystery Girl*.

1989

TOURING IN FRANCE, PAUL MCCARTNEY PERFORMS PLENTY OF SONGS FROM THE BEATLES REPERTOIRE...

ONE OF MY FRIENDS HAS DECORATED PAUL'S DRESSING ROOM WITH RECORDS BY MY BAND. I OFFER ONE TO LINDA WHEN I MEET HER IN THE WINGS.

IT'S YOU HERE !?!

LOGE

THANK YOU

GREAT !

JUST BEFORE THE CONCERT, PAUL RECOGNISES ME AND SAYS...

HEY! THE BANANA GUY! THANK YOU FOR THE RECORD !!!

HE PROBABLY DID A LOT OF OTHER THINGS THAT YEAR...

C BLAIS

Cnobba b CCCP

'Back In The USSR' in Russian. Paul is the first western artist to record an album for the Soviet market.

Declan MacManus, better known as Elvis Costello, co-writes several songs on Paul's new album. The two "Macs" also compose songs for *Spike*, the new album by the irascible Costello, among them the single 'Veronica', a big hit in the USA.

PAUL McCARTNEY
Flowers in the dirt

LP/June 89/Parlophone

This album, which should have marked the return of a Paul McCartney finally reassuming his role as a Beatle, was something of a disappointment. With Elvis Costello playing the part of a short-tempered alter ego in the manner of Lennon, it was going to be great. Well, it is the easiest on the ear album since *McCartney II*, but that's not saying much. Most of the songs are good, if not very good ('You Want Her Too'). But the majority are also dreadfully produced, with annoying synthesizers everywhere. Unfortunately, in 1989, the 1980s were not dead yet.
(The sleeve reproduced here is that of the Beatles-like single 'My Brave Face'.)

In the USSR, as in all countries in the Eastern block, rock music is forbidden. But Beatles bootlegs are to be found hidden in anonymous sleeves decorated with flowers, in case of a house search by the KGB.

"As far as I'm concerned, there won't be a Beatles reunion as long as John Lennon remains dead." George Harrison, 28/11/89.

McCARTNEY

If the Beatles had been more interested
in bananas than in strawberry fields,
they would have been called The Velvet
Underground and would have recorded the
other great record of 1967.

1990

Yves Chaland draws a graphic video promo of the song 'Revolution', imagining the surviving Beatles in 2010.

Tripping the live fantastic

From Wembley to Rio through Osaka and Liverpool, Paul McCartney's world tour has lasted nearly a year with around a hundred concerts. A live video and CD crown it.

91

AUNTIE MIMI

The strong and resourceful lady who raised John dies at the age of 85 at the house in Poole that her adopted son bought her in 1965 to escape from his fans. Every week until his death, John would phone Mimi to tell her his news.

TRAVELING WILBURYS Vol. 3

LP/October 90/Wilbury records

Vol. 3? Yes, it's George's idea, the missing Vol. 2 being perhaps Roy Orbison. His partners miss him, and the album too, which is less subtle than the first. But it is still pretty good, with enjoyable guitar parts and George's doleful voice. As for Dylan, he sounds more and more like a drunken duck. Is it me or does 'The Devil's Been Busy' sound like the Beatles 'Anytime At All'?

IF YOU LIKE THE BEATLES CIRCA 65-66, YOU WILL LIKE THIS LIVERPOOL BAND!

In 1989, cured of his thirst, Ringo launches the first world tour of his career, with his musician friends. A record is released in autumn 1990.

Stanislas and M. Bernard tell "THE STORY OF THE BEATLES" in comic form.

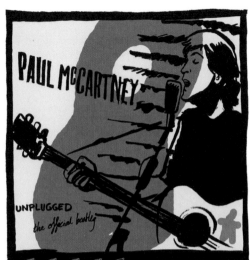

PAUL McCARTNEY
Unplugged (The official bootleg)

LP/May 91/Parlophone

This live album, the first of the series, was recorded on the January 25, 1991 during the *Unplugged* show on MTV. There are acoustic versions of Paul's songs, from the Beatles to his solo work, and a few old rock numbers like 'Be-Bop-A-Lula', all performed in good humour with a very "scouts campfire" ambiance. It is a relief to see Paul put away his synthesizers and play "roots", without effects. A curiosity in this live show: he sings 'I Lost My Little Girl', the first song he composed at the tender age of 14!

LIVERPOOL ORATORIO

An oratorio by Paul McCartney?
Well, yes! This one-hour 40-minute classical piece is commissioned for the 150th anniversary of the Royal Liverpool Orchestra. Assisted by Carl Davis (Paul still doesn't know musical theory let alone how to write music), this super kitsch oratorio was recorded in Liverpool Cathedral and released as a double CD.

"I knew the Beatles were angels on earth. I could never be upset with angels."
Maharishi Mahesh Yogi.

In the Netherlands, the Maharishi forgives a tearful George Harrison. They hadn't seen each other since the departure of the Beatles from Rishikesh, where the Maharishi supposedly made advances to Mia Farrow. It was a complete fabrication concocted by Magic Alex who wanted to get back to England. But it gave us the beautiful 'Sexy Sadie'.

ANTHOLOGY
A major documentary about the Beatles is launched. George doesn't like the original title The Long And Winding Road as he doesn't want the band to be summed up by Paul's song. A good start indeed.

92

KURT COBAIN

The leader of Nirvana declares himself a Beatles fan. Other alternative rock bands have covered the band's songs. Sonic Youth ('Within You...'), the Pixies ('Wild Honey Pie'). As for that oaf Bono (U2), he has the cheek to write a follow-up to Lennon's 'God'!

RINGO STARR
Time takes time

LP/May 92/Private music

Jeff Lynne's production ("Beatles for FM") obviously has something to do with it, as this comeback album by Ringo has a big sound fashioned on the Traveling Wilburys. A pseudo-Sixties ambience, some nice songs (like 'What Goes Around'). This is Ringo's best album since *Ringo* in 1973.

LINDA publishes a book gathering her best photographs from the Sixties, when she was taking pictures of rock stars.

GEORGE HARRISON with Eric Clapton
Live in Japan

LP/July 92/Dark horse

BEATLES GO BAROQUE
Peter Breiner
and
His Chamber Orchestra

93 My Ukulélé gently weeps

George is a big collector of guitars, dobros and other ukuleles. But his real passion is the banjo-ukulele, which he plays wonderfully well.

Baba Yaga covers 'Back In The USSR' in the manner of Slavic polyphonies.

ALWAYS ON THE LOOKOUT, PAUL MCCARTNEY RELEASES THIS (BORING) RECORD OF AMBIENT TECHNO TRANCE WITH THE BASS PLAYER AND PRODUCER YOUTH UNDER THE NAME THE FIREMAN.

Off the Ground

PAUL McCARTNEY
Off the ground

LP/February 93/Parlophone

Prefaced by the promising single 'Hope Of Deliverance', Paul's Off The Ground is simply the twin of his previous album Flowers In The Dirt. Except that the sound is less synthetic, which is good news. But too many soft ballads provoke untimely yawns. Contrary to what it says on the sleeve, we haven't been lifted off the ground.

Felix culpa !

Prefaced by the promising single 'Hope Of Deliverance', Paul's *Off The Ground* is simply the twin of his previous album Flowers In The Dirt. Except that the sound is less synthetic, which is good news. But too many soft ballads provoke untimely yawns. Contrary to what it says on the sleeve, we haven't been lifted off the ground.

PAUL McCARTNEY
Paul is live

LP/November 93/Parlophone

Nothing but routine. A new triumphant world tour, a new live album. An incredible repertoire treated all too often in a clumsy way. One surprise: a very good version of 'Looking For Changes', a song from *Off The Ground*, which is best played live and "ballsy".

Notice the sleeve and title, a response to "Paul is dead", (the number plate on the VW Beetle this time says "51 IS"). Yes, Paul is in his fifties now.

As for the dog, it is Arrow, one of the famous Martha's offspring.

The incredible Beatles Complete Scores transcribes the music for each instrument for all of the band's song.

FRANÇOIS ÀYROLES

94 THE THREETLES

In February, there is a crazy rumour. The three surviving Beatles are in the studio at Friar Park, George's home! They are recording old rock (standards) as well as new songs with Jeff Lynne as producer. A new album will coincide with the *Anthology*, the documentary series recounting the Beatles career, which will be broadcast the following year...

Oasis #2

Is it me or does 'Whatever' (number two in the British charts at Christmas) sound like 'All You Need Is Love' and 'All The Young Dudes' by Mott the Hoople?

NEW YORK

Harrison calls Paul to talk about supporting the Natural Law Party at the European elections. The NLP are associated with the Maharishi and his transcendental meditation. Paul answers evasively. George drops it.

* * *

Backbeat is a film that recounts the story of the Beatles in Hamburg.

* * *

The tapes of the mythical concert in Woolton, in 1957, are brought by EMI and Apple for £78,500 at an auction.

Paul and Yoko (with Linda and Sean Lennon, now 19) record an avant-garde piece, 'Hiroshima Sky'. But it remains under wraps.

'Live at the BBC'

THE BEATLES
Live at the BBC

2xLP/November 94/Apple

- -

Fifty-six songs and some chat recorded for the BBC between 1963 and 1965! A whole lot of covers and unreleased versions of the Fab Four's well-known songs. The BBC having kept only two of the Beatles recordings, fans who had pirated them at the time are asked to collaborate on the making of this record. A gargantuan album filled with the freshness of The Beatles early in their career, which is not always the case with historical albums like this. Within a year, it sells eight million copies!

And, by the way, the album is released on the Apple label, reinstated after 19 years of inactivity, under the control of their old friend Neil Aspinall.

THE DOCUMENTARY SERIES IS BROADCAST IN 94 COUNTRIES AND IS VERY SUCCESSFUL. 'THE BEATLES NARRATE THE BEATLES' IS AN EXCITING AND EXHAUSTIVE DOCUMENT DESTINED FOR POSTERITY.

Britpop!

Blur pose on the stairs of EMI, identical to the old ones but now in the company's new building at Hammersmith.

"Lennon was right. And we are bigger than Jesus. We will be as big as the Beatles, if not bigger."
(Liam Gallagher)

Oasis #2

The Beatles
Free As A Bird/Christmas Time

Single/December 95/Apple

From John Lennon's primitive demo, Jeff Lynne and the three survivors produce a kind of song. The montage doesn't work, the process is flawed, the result abysmal, and nobody with any sense will consider this a Beatles single.

It's astonishing that artists who in the past were so demanding have stooped to this.

THE MAHARISHI'S TRANSCENDENTAL MEDITATION ENTERS THE LIST OF APPROVED SECTARIAN ORGANISATIONS IN FRANCE AND THE USA.

THE BEATLES
Anthology 1

2 x LP/November 95/Apple

Finally the Beatles' unreleased songs appear after 25 years, on three double albums, this being the first, covering the period 1958-1964. After the uneasy opener 'Free As A Bird', the glimpses into the past are incredible: the acetate of the Quarrymen from 1958, songs with Stuart Sutcliffe, titles from the Decca audition, working versions of well-known songs, unreleased songs, live versions (among them the "jewels" from the Royal Variety Show). Musically it is inconsistent, and the early songs sound prehistoric to our 1995-tuned ears. We particularly appreciate the rockabilly version of 'One After 909', and the unreleased song 'Leave My Kitten Alone'.

But be careful. This obviously isn't the right way to start listening to the Beatles, and we don't particularly feel like listening to it over and over.

It is "for fans only" - but there are billions of them out there.

A Carlsberg advert broadcast during the first episode of the Anthology on British television: "Probably the Pete Best lager in the world."

96

"NOW AND THEN",

A third Lennon song, unreleased and now tampered with, is not included after all on volume three of the Anthology. George (here visiting the tomb of Saint Rupa Goswami in Vrindavan) thought the result mediocre and used his veto.

Oasis #3

The band has become a phenomenon in England, where it is voted best band of all time ahead of the Beatles in a poll! On another note, 'Setting Sun', by the Chemical Brothers with Noel Gallagher, is it me or does it sound like 'Tomorrow Never Knows'?

IF YOU LIKE THE BEATLES YOU MIGHT LIKE SUPERGRASS.

REAL ♥ LOVE

♫♫♫♫♫

The Beatles
Real Love/Baby's In Black

Single/March 96/Apple

- -

The second unreleased song by Lennon and now reworked by his comrades. It is slightly less mediocre than 'Free As A Bird' as the song itself is actually better.

Ringo, on the release of this single:
"Recording the new songs didn't feel contrived at all, it felt very natural and it was a lot of fun, but emotional too at times. But it's the end of the line, really. There's nothing more we can do as the Beatles."

To everyone's relief.

♫♫♫♫♫

THE BEATLES
Anthology 2

2 x LP/March 96/Apple

- -

The second volume of the *Anthology* is much more exciting than the first, enabling fans to experience again the genesis of the mythical songs from the 65-67 period, the Beatles golden era.

There are some unreleased titles on offer too, like 'That Means A Lot' and 'If You've Got Troubles!' Exciting documents, like that first take of 'Yesterday' or the instrumental version of 'Eleonor Rigby'! Live titles, Shea stadium '65 and the Budokan '66.

The second record is devoted mainly to Sgt Pepper, covering for example the long creative process of 'Strawberry Fields', from the superb acoustic demo to the intermediary versions before the montage.

A shame that we have to put up with 'Real Love', the song put together by the 'Threetles', and the sleeves of these anthologies, designed by Klaus Voorman, make us long for the sublime drawing he made for *Revolver*.

- -

Some businessmen offer $225 million to the three Beatles to go back on stage together. They refuse.

🎵🎵🎵🎵🎵

THE BEATLES
Anthology 3

2 x LP/November 96/Apple

Hey presto, the third and last volume of the *Anthology*, six months after the previous one. Once again the menu, concocted by George Martin and Mark Lewisohn, and re-mixed by Geoff Emerick, is copious. It covers the period 1968-69, from the White Album to the separation, and the painful sessions for 'Get Back'. Particularly notable are the acoustic demo of 'While My Guitar Gently Weeps', a very pretty and delicate 'She Came In Through The Bathroom Window' and lashings of unreleased songs, among them the famous 'What's The New Mary Jane', reminiscent of Syd Barrett.

Finally, was it really necessary to explore the mystery of the artists' vision by dwelling on sometimes dull work processes? Well, it's a bit late to ask that question now!

THE RUTLES

They also release their anthology named Archaeology!

97 Sir McCartney

On March 11, Paul, like George Martin a few months before, receives a knighthood from the Queen. The heroes of the Swinging Sixties have reached the right age for honours. And no medals were sent back as a sign of protest.

blur

'Beetlebum' by Blur! Beautiful as a Lennon!

beetlebum

PAUL McCARTNEY

🧦🧦🧦🤍🤍

Paul McCartney
Flaming Pie

LP/May 97/Parlophone

"Sit down there, kid. You know, what you're doing with your band, Oasis, it's no good. People buy it, right, but they know it's worth nothing. Shit. They will always prefer the original to the copy. I am releasing an album, and it's my best in 20 years. Well, it's not perfect, there are some clumsy blues, but it's well produced and there are three or four good songs on it. You see, listening again to those old songs for the *Anthology* has, how can I put it, given me back the taste. What I wanted to tell you, kid, is: make the most of your 15 minutes of fame. As for me, it's been going on for 34 years. And I won't let bushy eyebrowed little thugs like you put an end to it. Luigi, show the door to our young friend, I think he got the message."

Derek Taylor,

Derek Taylor, PR during the mad Apple years dies from cancer. He came back to work for the Beatles from 1993 to 1997.

98

Linda McCartney
1941-1998

Linda passes away in her Tucson ranch, in Arizona, with Paul at her side, after a three-year battle with cancer.

Vegetarian, activist for animal causes, she asked that her treatment had not been tested on animals.

99

HORROR!

On December 30 at 3a.m., George, in his Friar Park palace, is woken by the sound of broken glass. He goes down to investigate, and Michael Abram, 33, stabs him seven times, once in the lung. Olivia is also wounded in the struggle. The police intervene and arrest the man "on a mission from God". Harrison is hospitalised, but he recovers.

SEAN LENNON

Sean Lennon, 23, releases his first album on the Beastie Boys label, Grand Royal. A young man of his time, his album, very eclectic (from Bossa Nova to electronic grunge) is noticed. But his voice, though reminiscent of his father's mixed with the Teletubbies, lacks some bite. Not easy to be the "son of", but Sean copes reasonably well.

George,

George, who calls Paul "His Lordship" since his knighthood, announces he has completely recovered from the throat cancer that had considerably weakened him.

George has taken up musical activities again, and plays on Ringo's latest album.

RINGO STARR

Vertical Man, Ringo's eleventh album.

Threetles, last.

In July, Paul and George celebrate Ringo's 60th birthday. George, in a good mood, seems to have suffered no ill effects from the attack, even though he remains in his home most of the time now.

20 00

🥾🥾🥾🥾🥾

PAUL McCARTNEY
Run devil run
LP/October 99/Parlophone

- -

Linda's death has left its mark on Paul. After a year of mourning he decides to drown his sorrow by making, like John Lennon 24 years earlier, an album of rock standards. With a few old mates he makes some noise, bawls some Elvis and Big Joe Turner songs and writes three others in 1956 fashion. Since the passing of his wife Paul has aged, his features are sunken now. But this old teenager's album shows that the devil still has a few years running in him.

PS: Paul presents this new album in the reopened Cavern Club in Liverpool!

This record, compiling all the number ones by The Beatles, sells 12 million copies in three weeks!

A slightly laborious but not uninteresting experimental album by Paul McCartney, Youth and the Welsh band Super Furry Animals. A follow-up to 'Carnival Of Lights'? (See 1967).

liverpool sound collage

30 years later, the Yellow Sub reappears!

Oasis #4
Liam is the father of a little one...
Lennon Gallagher.

Bugman

Those two were going to meet sooner or later, for they are of the same breed – hyper-active, jack-of-all-trades musicians and genial pop songwriters. Paul lights Daman Albarn's cigarette during the very boozy ceremony at the *NME* Awards, February 1, 2000.

01

Crabe.

He was only in remission. In May, a tumour is removed from George's lung. In July, he undergoes radiotherapy for a brain tumour.

Exhausted, knowing it is the end, he devotes his final days to recording a new album with his son Dhani and Jeff Lynne.

HOLY BEABLE

The superb book version of the *Anthology* series is an indispensable document crammed with unpublished information and photos.

If you like Abbey Road, listen to Figure 8 by Elliott Smith.

RINGS AROUND THE WORLD

PAUL McCARTNEY
Driving rain
LP/November 01/Parlophone

An album that is unfairly neglected. His latest solo album is the hardest, the darkest and the most moving with McCartney still as creative and concerned about not repeating himself. A special mention to 'Spinning On An Axis', co-written with his son James, like Marvin Gaye traversed by a sick and grim riff.

And that vaguely Indian song, 'Riding Into Jaipur', is it a wink to his old mate who is ill?

The Magical Mystery Tour of the year 2000 with Paul as guest on the celery.

George Harrison

1943 - 2001

The various treatments and operations could do nothing. George passes away on November 29, 2001 at Hollywood Hills. His ashes are scattered in the Ganges, following Hindu tradition.

He was my little baby brother.
Paul McCartney.

As nothing in this life that I've been trying
Could equal or surpass the art of dying
George Harrison, in *'Art Of Dying'* (1970).

02

George hadn't finished his last album. But he left very precise written instructions to Dhani and Jeff Lynne. After much hard work, they succeed in completing George's work.

BRAINWASHED

by George Harrison

Here is the coat of arms of Macca the knight. His motto is: "ECCE COR MEUM" (Here's My Heart).

Sir Paul McCartney marries Heather Mills, a 35 year-old ex-model, whose left leg has been amputated following an accident.

***

Paul has the famous "Lennon-McCartney" changed into "McCartney-Lennon" on the Beatles songs he composed alone like 'Blackbird', embarrassing himself before his fans.

YOKO buys the house on **Menlove Avenue** where **John Lennon** grew up and donates it to the **National Trust.**

Concert for George

On November 29, a tribute concert is organised at the Royal Albert Hall. Paul, Ringo, Clapton, Dhani, Billy Preston, Ravi Shankar and many others perform George's songs in front of 5,000 people, all of them very moved.

CLAPTON

GEORGE HARRISON
Brainwashed

LP/November 02/Dark horse

- -

One year after his death, George Harrison's posthumous album is released. He began work slowly, as early as 1988, but with his disease taking hold he doubled his efforts in the last few months, still working in the studio the day before his (final) departure for Los Angeles, in November 2001.
It is completed and produced by Jeff Lynne, whose influence is recognizable, Brainwashed is neither the best nor the worst of Harrison's albums. But listening to it is a pleasure, one is moved by his tired voice and by some beautiful passages, like the final Hindu prayer sung in unison with Dhani.

George, who was notoriously deadpan, had a very peculiar sense of humour. Knowing he was terminally ill, he called his new production company "RIP".

- -

George Harrison's attacker is released on probation 19 months after being imprisoned.

03

Heather gives birth to Beatrice, Paul McCartney's fourth child. Far from demoralized by the commercial disappointment of his excellent Driving Rain, Paul, now 61, embarks on another of the huge world tours that he enjoys so much.

back to the world

Best (off)

Pete Best, 62, narrowly avoids a bad accident in the coach used by his Pete Best Band.

After having been ousted by The Beatles, he remained a musician for a while, then became a baker and then worked for the Royal Mail until his retirement. Credited and therefore remunerated for playing on 10 songs on the *Anthology*, he no longer deserves the title "the unluckiest man on earth"!

789th album for Ringo who once again elevates monotony to the status of major art.

The copy of Double Fantasy signed by Lennon for Mark Chapman is sold for $850,000. Chapman's anticipated release is refused. At the same time, a price has been put on his head in several countries

81 A38360 CHAPMAN, MARK D

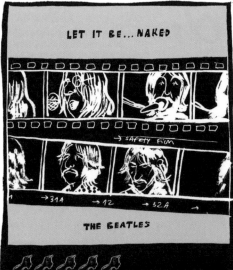

LET IT BE... NAKED

→ SAFETY FILM

→ 31A   → 12   → 32A   →

THE BEATLES

♫♫♫♫♫

THE BEATLES
Let it be...Naked

LP/November 2003/Apple

- -

Paul McCartney sees it as his duty to deal with the Beatles heritage.

It is no secret that the album Let It Be, arranged by Allen Klein and Phil Spector, has been a bugbear of Paul's since it was first released (see 1970).

At the beginning of 2002, he instructs Abbey Road engineers to de-Spectorise the album using the 30 recording tapes from the 'Get Back' sessions. And, while they are at it, to re-mix and re-master the lot.

Out go the violins, the extracts of dialogue, the bits of unfinished songs. It's a clean sweep and Lennon's great song 'Don't Let Me Down' (B-side of the single 'Get Back') is added.

Some call it cultural revisionism. Okay, fair enough. But the result is superb! Guitar-bass-drums. A bit of organ by Billy Preston. And good songs. Nothing else.

Apart from that, the title is rubbish and the sleeve too.

04 The Grey Album

Fascinating and absurd! Danger Mouse mixes Jay-Z's Black Album with the White Album with no authorisation whatsoever! EMI has the record withdrawn.

The band Beatallica interprets Beatles songs in the manner of Metallica. Hilarious!

***

Is it me or does Frank Ferdinand's 'Take Me Out' sound like Ringo's 'Back Off Boogaloo'?

***

'Ob-La-Di, Ob-La-Da' voted worst song of all time in a poll published on BBC News.

A wonderful book in which Paul opens up about his life. We learn (among other things) that, as teenagers, he and John Lennon had wanking competitions!

BARRY MILES

PAUL McCART[NEY]

MANY TEARS FRO[M]

05

George Martin has suggested genius producer

Nigel Godrich

to Paul for his next album. Macca has been producing almost all his records alone since 1977.

The producer of Radiohead, Beck and many others is known for his intransigence. Paul hadn't been rocked like that since when John was around.

Chaos & creation at Abbey Road

On July 28, in front of an audience of lucky bastards, Paul, in a witty mood, performs a dozen songs alone with mellotron, double bass, a glass...

PAUL McCARTNEY
Chaos & creation in the backyard

LP/September 05/Parlophone

What motivates a man like Paul McCartney? Why does he still produce albums regularly? Why those tours, all that activity? At 63, doesn't he deserve to rest, to contemplate his monumental work with the satisfaction of having done his duty?

Yes, but the problem is that McCartney has always been the most "musicianly" and the most ambitious of the Beatles. That's the thing. In 2005, he still wants to prove he's the best, and anyway, this bloke composes ALL THE TIME.

But this time, the young dandy Godrich has put a spoke in his wheels. He is forbidden to call on his usual session musicians. He will have to play all the instruments, as in 1970.

Godrich has also rejected half of Paul's new songs, imposed great moderation in orchestration, and forced him to not fall back on his old clichés.

One can only imagine the look on the face of the living legend and the sometimes tense atmosphere in the studio. But Macca has trusted his young collaborator.

And the result is magnificent.

On February 6, during the Super Bowl Final, Paul performs four songs in front of a billion viewers!

06

Billy Preston, one of the 'fifth Beatles', passes away. After playing on *Get Back* he toured with the Rolling Stones and enjoyed a great career.

07

On October 9, the Imagine peace tower, a vertical laser on Viey Island in Iceland, is switched on in the presence of Yoko, Ringo and Olivia.

TriBute-Bands

With violin basses, vintage wigs and Cuban-heeled boots, there are apparently at least 130 bands in the world performing the Beatles repertoire note for note, all of them successful. A few examples:

The Bootleg Beatles (UK)
The Brothers (Argentina)
The Buggs (USA, as early as 1965)
The Fab Faux (USA, no wigs)
Les Rabeats (France)
Silver Beats (Japan)

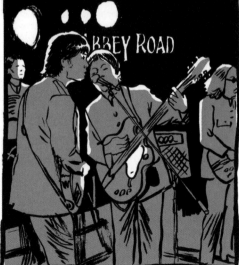

Oasis #5

Zak Starkey, Ringo's son, becomes the band's drummer! (see 1965)

A compilation on which the Beatles songs are all mixed up in a completely idiotic fashion.

Eh! A new album by Ringo! But wait, hasn't he released this one already?

The Great Divorce

Heather and Paul separate with much ado. After an acrimonious court case, she is awarded £23 million.

Fans of her ex send her death threats.

★★★★★

PAUL McCARTNEY
Memory almost full

LP/June 07/MPL-Hear

- -

Godrich is a good kid. We made a fine album, and the critics were unanimous. But, you know, the critics... *Sgt Pepper*, it was me, see what I mean. And then, it didn't sell very well, did it? And it made me feel old, on top of that. But you know, I am not an old nostalgic Beatle, I am a pop singer in the year 2000. So I'm telling you what we're going to do. The songs the little squirt has dared to refuse, we're going to do them. I call on my usual musicians, I play in stadiums with them, they are cool guys, you see. And let's put an end to analogue sound and to moderation too, and instead let's use filters, big drums, choruses like Queen and synthesizers everywhere to make it all nice and heavy, and then let's format it all for the radio. And here we go again, for another 45 years. Muse and Black Eyed Peas, just watch out, Paul won't let go.

PS: In 'Vintage Clothes', Paul makes fun of youngsters who dress in clothes from the past. Must live with your time, guys. But the costumes on *Sgt Pepper*, what was it all about then?

After 45 years, Paul leaves EMI for Hear Music, the Starbucks label!

08 Deaths of the Maharishi and Neil Aspinall, their friend from Liverpool, assistant to the Beatles since 1963 and boss of Apple from 1968 to 2007.

On July 20, 2008, Paul McCartney plays a big free concert on the Plains of Abraham during the 400th anniversary celebrations of the city of Quebec.

Yesstaday, all ma truballs seemd so fare away! Naw it louks az thoo der ere to stay!

Unfortunately, the 200,000 spectators know all his repertoire.

Peace & love

On his site, Ringo pleads with his fans to stop sending him mail.

"Nothing will be signed after October 20. If that is the date on the envelope, it's gonna be tossed."

In *Chapter 27*, Jared Leto plays the part of Mark Chapman.

The Catcher In The Rye has 26 chapters (see 1980).

HAYMANS GREEN

A tribute band whose second drummer is the old Pete Best. Somewhere between the Rutles in bad shape and Tears for Fears circa 89.

THE PETE BEST BAND

11 years after John's, George Harrison's star is inaugurated on the famous Hollywood Walk Of Fame on Vine Street.

THE VATICAN ANNOUNCES THAT IT 'FORGIVES' JOHN LENNON FOR HIS FAMOUS STATEMENT 43 YEARS AGO, BLAMING IT ON THE FACT THAT HE WAS "A YOUNG WORKING-CLASS ENGLISHMAN FACED WITH UNEXPECTED SUCCESS". WHEN WILL HE BE CANONIZED?

The Plastic Ono Band is resurrected by Yoko and Sean.

09

MASTER!

It's advertised everywhere. Re-mastered versions of the Beatles albums are now available. There is even a box set of mono versions (considered the best). They are bought en masse, and 11 albums by the Fab Four are in the British Top 40. At number one is a best of Vera Lynn album, a star from the Forties, who, at 92, could be Ringo's mother.

Patrick Eudeline, in Rock & Folk, sums it up: 'You may as well buy old second-hand vinyl, it's cheaper, it's more beautiful and the sound is really good.'

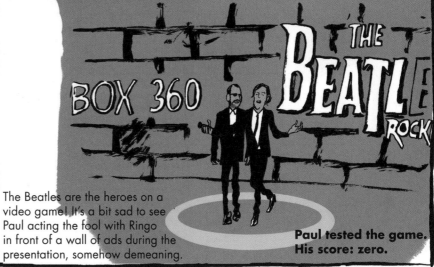

The Beatles are the heroes on a video game! It's a bit sad to see Paul acting the fool with Ringo in front of a wall of ads during the presentation, somehow demeaning.

Paul tested the game. His score: zero.

Patrimonial?

Some 50 years after the formation of the band, 40 years after its split, the Beatles are still a gold mine (official shops appear everywhere, the compilation 1 was the best selling album in the first decade after 2000). They are a venerable institution. We lose count of the honours, the exhibitions or museums devoted to the band or to John Lennon... A masters degree course in the Beatles and Popular Music has even been created at Liverpool Hope University.

I still love "The Beatles"

"I'm Paul, from Rock Band©"

That's how McCartney introduces himself in January 2010 at the Grammy Awards.

In June, his tour bus comes under attack in Mexico. But the police intervene, and they are more frightened than hurt.

At 68, one of the 10 wealthiest Brits (around $1 billion), Paul never talks about stopping touring, and announces a new album soon.

"Like Daddy"

Sean replays Annie Leibowitz' famous photo, with the roles reversed. It's a bit facile.

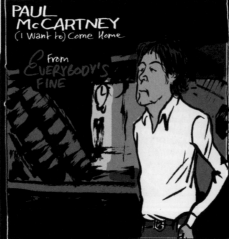

PAUL McCARTNEY
(I Want to) Come Home
From EVERYBODY'S FINE

🎵🎵🎵🎵🎵

**PAUL McCARTNEY
(I want to) come home**

MP3/December 09/MPL

A song available only as a download, composed for Robert de Niro's latest film, at his request. It's a sentimental ballad pitched somewhere between 'The Long And Winding Road' and 'We Are The World'. "Classic Macca," as one says. And that should be enough, for sure.

RINGO STARR

Y NOT

Isn't a new album by Ringo Starr a wonderful way to conclude this book?

On December 10, 2009, I saw Paul McCartney at Bercy. It was the first time I have seen a real Beatle in person. By "I saw" I mean... I glimpsed him, let's say, I was not in the best seat. It was very expensive, but it was very good. Except for the violins on 'Eleanor Rigby' played on a synthesizer...

An anecdote: although I felt moved, I didn't cry. I felt just the opposite the following week during 'All My Loving', performed by the Rabeats, a tribute-band in concert at the Femina in Bordeaux.

There is nothing to understand or conclude from that.

SOURCES

BOOKS

Eight days a Week, by Robert Whitaker & Marcus Hearn (2008, Reynolds & Hearn)
En studio avec les Beatles, by Geoff Emerick & Howard Massey (2009, Le mot et le reste)
Imagine John Lennon, by Andrew Solt & Sam Ergan (1989, Albin Michel)
John Lennon / interviews de Playboy, by David Sheff (1982, Générique)
Les Beatles, by Jacques Volcouve et Pierre merle (1987, Solar)
McCartney, by Jacques Volcouve & Michel Dubreuil (1989, Ergo press)
Paul McCartney, by Barry Miles (2004, Flammarion)
Revolution Les Beatles, by Jacques Volcouve & Pierre Merle (1998, Fayard)
Rock&Folk interviews (1979, Humanoïdes associés / Speed 17)
Souvenir des Beatles, by Har Van Fulpen (1983, Artefact)
The Beatles anthology, traduit par Philippe Paringaux (2000, Seuil)
The Beatles Day By Day, by Mark Lewisohn (1990, Harmony books)
The Beatles Get Back, by Russell, Cott & Dalton (1969, Apple Publishing)
The Beatles' London, by Piet Shreuders, Mark Lewisohn & Adam Smith (1994, Portico)
The Beatles On Camera, by Mark Hayward (2009, Pavilion)
The Beatles Unseen Archives, by Tim Hill & Marie Clayton (2000, Paragon)
The Complete Beatles Recording Sessions, by Mark Lewisohn (1988, EMI / Hamlyn)

MAGAZINES

Beatles Book Monthly # 9, 20, 35, 37, 38, 41, 46, 47, 61, 68, 75
Les Inrockuptibles # 294
Mojo # 108, 114, 121
Mojo limited, 1000 days that shook the world
NME originals The Beatles / The solo years / John Lennon
Rock&Folk # 118
The Fab Four publication # 25

DVD

Classic Albums : Plastic Ono Band (2008, Eagle vision)
Imagine John Lennon (1988, Warner)
The McCartney Years (2007, Mpl / Warner)
The Beatles Anthology (2003, Abbey Road interactive / Apple)

Websites

www.beatles.com
www.beatlesource.com
www.georgeharrison.com
http://kenwoodlennon.blogspot.com
www.maccablog.com
www.paulmccartney.com
www.rateyourmusic.com
www.ringostarr.com
www.yellowsub.net

STONES
ou
BEATLES?

(A debate that has raged since 1964)

BIOGRAPHY

Hervé Bourhis was born in Touraine in 1974 and now lives in Bordeaux. Although *Le Petit Livre Rock* (Dargaud, 2007) made him known to the public, he is actually the author of a dozen graphic novels since he started working as an illustrator and a scriptwriter in 2002.

His work explores the sensations he experienced as a young reader. In *Comix Remix* (Dupuis) he revisits the naïve stories of the first Marvel super-heroes he used to read in *Strange*. In *Ingmar* (Dupuis), he creates, in collaboration with Rudy Spiessert, a kind of modern acid Johan and Pirlouit. Together they revisit *Star Wars in Naguère* (Delcourt).

But he's also interested in contemporary subjects. In La Main Verte (Futuropolis, 2009), he enjoys depicting a world without crude oil, while *Un Enterrement de Jeune Fille* (Dupuis, 2008) is an existential road movie with a female character. Hervé Bourhis received the Goscinny Prize in 2002 for his first graphic novel, *Thomas ou le Retour de Tabou*, a book about Boris Vian, whose biography he also wrote with Christian Cailleaux under the pseudonym Piscine Molitor.

He is also an illustrator and scriptwriter for cartoons and works regularly for events in the music world. In 2010 Hervé Bourhis was awarded the Jacques Lob Prize for his work.